哈福

哈福

旅美英語作家專為華人寫的

# 流利英語
# 必備句型

## Upgrade Your English
培養英語實力，從基本句型開始！

SCAN

附QR碼線上音檔
互動學習 即刷即聽

蘇盈盈 ◎著

哈福

# 學好基本句型，英語高人一等！

　　要學會説流利的英語，基本句型是很重要的一環，因為語言就是由每一個句子所組成，句子集結文字，譜出流暢的話語，構成最自然的英語會話！

　　有鑑於此，本書完全跳脱字典的制式範例，特別收錄日常生活中最常用的106個句型，讀者不但能夠增加表達能力，同時也能認識到所學單字在日常生活會話中的實際功用。

　　為了方便您了解整個句型的特色及用法，每個句型由5個單元分類解説：「句型模擬站」裡的基礎句型、「句型解析站」中關於句子正確用法的説明、字義辨別及易犯的錯誤、「句型連結站」單元裡靈活運用的各項造句、正式交談就能靈活運用的「會話廣播站」，以及「單字片語加油站」，為您列出文章中的常用單字，加上這些在英文句中應注意的註解，使您説起英文更純正、更有信心！

　　熟記句型，就能靈活連結會話，並且應用在任何場合、任何談話主題，將雜亂無章的枝節片語，轉化成口若懸河的生動對談。本書帶著您完全解脱破英文的窘境，快速提升為流暢説英語的國際族群！

# ◆目錄◆

◆目錄◆

# ◆目錄◆

◆目 錄◆

# *001*

# **What did you think of~**

你認為…如何？

MP3-2

句型 模擬站

**What did you think of** the concert?
你認為那場音樂會如何？

### 句型解析站

　　本句型是天天必用的句型，但也是國人常犯錯誤的句型，問題出在國人在詢問別人意見時，是問意見「如何」？而背英文生字的時候，「如何」這個字是how，所以不論是說話、寫作或考試，一看「如何」就直覺地代入how，而不知道用what。現在你知道what did you think of 的意思和易犯錯原因，保證下回不會再犯錯了吧！英語實力要這樣才會進步！

　　　注意本句型用過去式did，表示所問的事已經發生過了。若是與時間無關，則可用現在式do，成為What do you think of ~? 的句型。

句型 連結站

What did you think of the concert?
你認為那場音樂會如何？

What did you think of the baseball game?
你認為那一場棒球賽如何？

What do you think of his new job?
你對他的新工作看法如何？

- ☑ concert
  ['kɑnsɝt]
  音樂會

- ☑ baseball
  ['bes,bɔl]
  棒球

- ☑ game
  [gem]
  比賽

- ☑ symphony
  ['sɪmfənɪ]
  交響樂

- ☑ relaxing
  [rɪ'læksɪŋ]
  精神放鬆

## 會話 轉播站

**A** I tried to call you last night.

**B** John and I went to the symphony.

**A** Oh, **what did you think of** the concert?

**B** The music was great.
It was very relaxing.

A 我昨天晚上一直試著打電話給你。

B 約翰和我昨天去聽管絃樂。

A 噢，你認為那一場音樂會如何？

B 音樂很棒。
非常輕鬆。

# **002** It feels like

它感覺上像是…

## 句型 模擬站

**It feels like it is cotton.**
它的質感像是棉的。

### 句型解析站

feel的原意是「感覺」，還記得文法上稱為「感官動詞」，屬「不完全不及物動詞」之一，後面要接形容詞或名詞作主詞補語嗎？

你八成不記得了吧！沒關係，英文法中有太多專有名詞，我們若是說話時，還要去想這些，對方一定看你魂不守舍，兩眼直視，一副快要發瘋的樣子，哪還有心情與你談下去呢？說了這麼多，是要告訴你，這個句型本與文法書無關，注意feel like加子句，表示「感覺上像是～」，這與中文說法一模一樣，英語其實不難啦！

## 句型 連結站

**It feels like it is marble.**
它的質感像是大理石的。

**It feels like she has fever.**
感覺起來她好像在發燒。

**It feels like it is silk.**
它的質感像是絲質的。

**A** What do you think this dress is made of?

**B** It **feels like** it is cotton.
What does the label say?

**A** It's missing.
I think you are right.
Do you think it is 100% cotton?

**B** Probably.

A 你看這套衣服是用什麼做的？

B 它感覺起來像是棉質的。
標籤上怎麼說？

A 標籤不見了。
我想你是對的。
你看是100%的棉嗎？

B 也許吧。

☑ cotton
[kɑtn̩]
棉花

☑ fever
[ˈfivɚ]
發燒

☑ silk
[sɪlk]
絲

☑ be made of
由～做成

☑ label
[ˈlebl̩]
標籤

☑ missing
[ˈmɪsɪŋ]
不見了

☑ probably
[ˈprɑbəblɪ]
可能地

# *003*

# May I ~?

## 我可以嗎…？

## May I go?
我可以走了嗎？

### 句型解析站

　　May I ~? 這個句型許多國人都自認會用；中學老師說，問人家「可不可以」做某件事，要用 May I ~ 的句型。問題是有多少人脫口而出的都是 Can I ~?

　　到底 Can I 是否正確呢？一般英美人士不會挑你毛病，不過總會有些調皮的人，要找你麻煩。你若是不用 May I 而用 Can I，他就回答 How should I know?（我怎麼知道？）本來嘛。英語 I can drive. 是「我會開車。」，那 Can I drive?是「我會開車嗎？」，既然你自己都不知道會不會開車，當然調皮的人就會回答 How should I know? 。你看，一字之差，多沒面子，所以，記住問人家的許可時，務必用 May I ~?。

### 句型 連結站

## May I have your attention, please?
請大家注意一下。

## May I have a look at the annual report?
我能看看你的年度報表嗎？

# May I borrow your car?
我能借你的車嗎?

## 會話 轉播站

**A** Mom, **may I** go over to Mary's house?

**B** It's getting late.
Have you finished your home-work?

**A** Yes, please, **may I** go?

**B** As long as you're home in time for dinner.

---

A 媽,我可以到瑪麗家嗎?

B 天快要黑了。
你所有的功課做完了沒有?

A 我都做完了。我可以去了嗎?

B 只要你及時回家吃晚飯就可以。

☑ attention
[ə'tɛnʃən]
注意

☑ annual
['ænjʊəl]
每年的;一年的

☑ report
[rɪ'port]
報告

☑ homework
['hom,wɜk]
家庭作業

☑ finish
['fɪnɪʃ]
做完

☑ as long as
只要

☑ go over to~
到~去

MP3-5

# What I don't understand is ~

我所不能理解的是…。

**What I don't understand is** why it is taking so long.

我所不能理解的是為什麼等這麼久。

## 句型解析站

本句型表示「難以理解」。what 是指某件事，I don't understand 是「不能理解」，is 之後才是詳細說明到底是哪件事難以理解。這種句型構造，還可以把動詞 understand更改成別的字，例如 agree（同意），用以表示「我所不能同意的是」哪件事。請看下面的例句。

## 句型 連結站

What I don't understand is why you are always late for work.

我所不能理解的是，為什麼你上班老是遲到？

What I don't agree with you is on the quality, not the price.

我與你看法相左的是品質，而不是價格。

What I don't like is when you dozed off at the meeting.
我所不喜歡的是你在會議中打瞌睡。

☑ quality
['kwɑlətɪ]
品質

☑ price
[praɪs]
價格

☑ doze
[doz]
打瞌睡

☑ doze off
打瞌睡

☑ meeting
['mitɪŋ]
會議

☑ service
['sɝvɪs]
服務

☑ restaurant
['rɛstərənt]
飯店

☑ slow
[slo]
慢的

☑ order
['ɔrdɚ]
點菜

☑ busy
['bɪzɪ]
忙的

## 會話 轉播站

A The service at this restaurant is slow!

B Really! We ordered our food almost twenty minutes ago.

A **What I don't understand is** why it is taking so long.
They are not very busy.

B Now we know why they aren't busy.
They're too slow!

A 這家餐館的服務真慢!

B 真的!我們點菜幾乎都快要20分鐘了。

A 我所不能理解的是,為什麼那麼久。
他們又不是很忙。

B 現在我們曉得為什麼他們不會很忙了。
他們的服務太慢了嘛!

# *005* This is great ~ weather.

## 這是個⋯的好天氣。

## This is great bike riding weather.

這是個騎腳踏車的好天氣。

### 句型解析站

　　學英語怎麼能不真槍實彈地上場與英美等國際友人面對面比劃比劃？本句是對初見面的人藉故搭訕的好句子，挨到他身邊，看他做什麼事，就說 This is great ~ weather. 把他正在做的事擺到~的位置，例如他在放風箏 (fly a kite) ，就說 This is great kite flying weather. 保證他一定要 Yes., Yeah., Sure.,You are right. 個沒完，你們這樣就一來一往，聊起來了。

### 句型 連結站

This is great kite flying weather.
這是個放風箏的好天氣。

This is great swimming weather.
這是個游泳的好天氣。

This is great golfing weather.
這是個打高爾夫的好天氣。

**A** Why don't we all go for bike riding and picnic?

**B** That's a great idea.
It shouldn't be too hot today.

**A** The forecast is for cool weather all day.

**B** **This is great** bike riding **weather**.

A 我們何不出去騎腳踏車並且野餐呢？

B 那是個好主意。
今天應該不會很熱。

A 氣象預告說，今天一整天都會很涼爽。

B 這真是個騎腳踏車的好天氣。

☑ weather
['wɛðɚ]
天氣

☑ kite
[kaɪt]
風箏

☑ golf
[gɑlf]
高爾夫球

☑ picnic
['pɪknɪk]
野餐

☑ bike
[baɪk]
腳踏車

☑ forecast
[for'kæst]
天氣預測

# 006

# To start with, ~

首先，…

MP3-7

**To start with**, she is wonderful with children.

首先，她這個人對小孩子非常好。

## 句型解析站

To start with是表示「首先」的意思。它都是用在句子的最前面，是起頭語。當別人問起什麼事，你擺出一副聽我「娓娓道來」的架勢時，第一句話就是To start with。注意這裡要用with，不要只說To start.。中文通常不用介係詞with，所以翻譯成英語時，很容易漏了。

## 句型 連結站

To start with, it was a gorgeous day.

首先，今天是一個大好的天氣。

To start with, the company is going out of business.

先說第一項吧，這個公司就要倒閉了。

To start with, the price is too high.
首先，這個價錢太高了。

☑ children
['tʃɪldrən]
小孩子

☑ gorgeous
['gɔrdʒəs]
很好的

☑ go out of business
結束營業

☑ enjoy
[ɪn'dʒɔɪ]
喜歡

**會話　轉播站**

**A** Why do you think Ms. Chen is a good teacher?

**B** **To start with**, she is wonderful with children.

**A** She seems to deal with them well.

**B** The other part is she enjoys the children.

A 你為何認為陳小姐是個好老師？

B 首先，她對小孩子非常好。

A 她似乎對小孩子很有一套。

B 另外一件事是，她喜歡跟小孩子在一起。

# *007*

## Really?

真的嗎？

MP3-8

## Really? How does he like it?

真的嗎？他還喜歡嗎？

---

### 句型解析站

　　Really? 的說法實在很常用，但國人不懂就不會用。當別人說話時，我們為了表示禮貌，不是經常雖心不在焉，沒有在聽，但卻猛點頭，假裝注意力很集中嗎？

　　是的，Really? 就有這種取代點頭的功能，不過要是語氣用錯了，就變成在反質問對方「真的嗎？」，好像一副對方胡說吹牛的樣子。所以你看，Really? 的後面，都有句子表示我真的在聽你說話，免得對方覺得說了半天，你還不信，那就有些「※○＊！」了。

---

### 句型 連結站

Really? How does she like the trip?
真的嗎？她還喜歡這趟旅行嗎？

Really? How do you like your new boss?
真的嗎？你覺得你的新老闆還可以嗎？

Really? What is his response to it?
真的嗎？他的反應如何？

單字　片語加油站

☑ really
　['riəlɪ]
　真的

☑ response
　[rɪ'spɑns]
　反應

☑ transfer
　[træns'fɝ]
　調換

會話　轉播站

**A** I just got a letter from John.
He was transferred to Hawaii.

- - - - - - - - - - - - - - - - - - - - - - -

**B** **Really**?　How does he like it?

- - - - - - - - - - - - - - - - - - - - - - -

**A** He says it's great.
But he hasn't had time to do a lot.

- - - - - - - - - - - - - - - - - - - - - - -

**B** It must be nice to live there.

- - - - - - - - - - - - - - - - - - - - - - -

A 我剛接到約翰來的一 信。
他被調到夏威夷去了。

B 真的嗎？他還喜歡嗎？

A 他說非常好。
但是他說他沒有時間做其他事情。

B 住在夏威夷一定很好。

# 008

## Does he like ~?

他喜歡…嗎？

MP3-9

**Does he like** wearing uniforms to school?

他喜歡穿制服上學嗎？

### 句型解析站

　　like這個字有表示「好像」的用法，如同第二單元中的 feel like所解釋的；它也有表示「喜歡」的意思，該如何分別呢？

　　　表示「喜歡」時，不會加在is、am、are、was、 were等的後面，而問別人「是否喜歡」時，一定由Do、 Does、Did、Will、Would這種字來起首。這樣分別，就簡單啦！

### 句型 連結站

Do you like wearing earrings to swimming?

你喜歡戴耳環游泳嗎？

Does he like carrying the briefcase to office?

他喜歡提手提箱上班嗎？

Do you like buying at big discount stores?
你喜歡從大的折扣店買東西嗎？

## 會話 轉播站

**A** **Does your** son **like** wearing uniforms to school?

**B** I don't think he really thinks about it.

**A** It must be hard to recognize him in a crowd of kids.

**B** No, he's easy to recognize at school.
He's the one with a crowd of girls trying to get his attention.

A 你兒子喜歡穿制服上學嗎？

B 我認為他不是很關心穿著。

A 要從一群小孩認出他一定很困難。

B 不，在學校他是很容易認出來的。
有一群小女生圍著要引起他注意的那個小男生，就是他。

☑ wear
[wɛr]
穿

☑ uniform
['junə,fɔrm]
制服

☑ earring
['ɪr,rɪŋ]
耳環

☑ carry
['kærɪ]
攜帶

☑ briefcase
['brif,kes]
手提箱

☑ discount
['dɪskaʊnt]
打折

☑ store
[stor]
商店

☑ recognize
['rɛkəg,naɪz]
認出

☑ crowd
[kraʊd]
一群人

☑ attention
[ə'tɛnʃən]
注意

# 009

# - what do you expect?

## …你還期望什麼？

### 句型 模擬站

## It's a rough road - **what do you expect?**
路這麼顛簸，你還期望什麼？

### 句型解析站

　　本句型常常用，但請注意，不要對初見面的人使用，就有點魯莽啦。但是對熟朋友、同學、情侶、同事、家人之間，那就請多多應用，在對方抱怨的時候，叫對方「免指望，斷了抱怨的念頭吧！」。

　　說了What do you expect?之後，要是有一種「你看我都不會亂抱怨！」的優越快感，那你說這句話的語氣就必定是對的了！

### 句型 連結站

## It's a tough job - what do you expect?
工作這麼難做，你還期望什麼？

## He's still young - what do you expect?
他還很年輕，你還期望怎樣？

I have tried my best - what do you expect?

我都已經盡了我的力了，你還期望怎樣？

## 會話 轉播站

**A** My whole body is starting to hurt with all this bouncing.

**B** It's a rough road - **what do you expect**?

**A** I don't know.
I think it has gotten a lot worse since the last time we were here.

**B** The county should pave it as soon as possible.

---

A 這樣抖動，我全身都開始痛了。

B 路這麼顛簸，你還期望怎樣？

A 我不知道。
自從我們上一次到這裡來，我看是越來越糟糕。

B 縣政府應該趕快把路鋪設起來。

☑ rough
[rʌf]
顛簸的

☑ tough
[tʌf]
困難

☑ whole
[hol]
整個

☑ hurt
[hɝt]
痛

☑ bouncing
['baʊnsɪŋ]
上下振動

☑ county
['kaʊntɪ]
縣

☑ pave
[pev]
鋪（路）

☑ possible
['pasəb!]
可能的

# I can't ~

我不能…

## 句型 模擬站

**I can't do this.**

我不能這麼做。

### 句型解析站

I can't 這個句型有兩種含意，一是能力不足，不會做，另一是「不為也，非不能也。」。例如一般說 I can't read.是「我不識字，不能看書。」；說 I can't do it. 可能就是「我不做！」了。

## 句型 連結站

I can't swim.
我不會游泳。

Can you play the piano?
你會彈鋼琴嗎？

I can't let you do it by yourself.
我不能讓你獨自做這件事情。

**A** I can't do this.
It's too hard.

---

**B** You can do this.
You have been working on
problems like this all year.

---

**A** But, these are harder.

---

**B** Look, if the company didn't think
you could do the work, you
wouldn't have been chosen for
the job.

---

☑ by yourself
你獨自一人

☑ hard
[hɑrd]
困難

☑ problem
[ˈprɑbləm]
問題

☑ harder
[ˈhɑrdɚ]
更困難（hard的
比較級）

☑ chosen
[ˈtʃozn̩]
挑選；選中
（choose的過去
分詞）

A 這件事情我無法做。
太困難了。

B 你可以做的。
你一整年都在解決像這樣的困難。

A 不過，這些更困難。

B 這樣說吧，如果公司不認為你可以做這樣的
事，你是不會被選來做這一份工作的。

# 011

# It's not ~; it's ~

不是⋯的問題；而是⋯

MP3-12

**It's not** the length that bothers me; **it's** the content.

困擾我的不是長度，而是內容。

### 句型解析站

本句型是兩句合成一句，所以中間以分號 "；" 標開。前部分用It's not 起始表示「非是原因所在」，後句用肯定式it's 點出真正原因。

這裡的例句都用 that bothers me（困擾我）來說明遭到困擾，但說話時，只要對方可以瞭解你的語意，不用也可以。例如上方的句子可以簡化成 It's not the length; it's the content. 意思還是完整的。

### 句型 連結站

It's not his work that bothers me; it's his attitude.

困擾我的不是他的工作，而是他的態度。

It's not the rain that bothers me; it's the wind.

困擾我的不是雨，而是風。

It's not the words of the song that bothers me; it's the noise.

困擾我的不是歌的歌詞，而是樂曲的噪音。

☑ length
  [lɛŋkθ]
  長度

☑ bother
  ['bɑðɚ]
  困擾

☑ content
  ['kɑntɛnt]
  內容

☑ attitude
  ['ætətjud]
  態度

☑ wind
  [wɪnd]
  風

☑ violence
  ['vaɪələns]
  暴力

**會話 轉播站**

**A** I really don't like this book.

**B** Neither do I.
  It is too long.

**A** **It's not** the length that bothers me; it's the content.
  There's too much violence.

**B** You're right about that.

A 我真的不喜歡這本書。

B 我也不喜歡。
  太長了。

A 叫我受不了的不是長度，而是內容。
  裏面有太多暴力了。

B 你的看法很正確。

# *012*

## ~ sounds like ~

那聽起來好像…的樣子。

句型 模擬站

## That **sounds like** fun.

那聽起來，好像很好玩的樣子。

### 句型解析站

本句 sound like 和第二單元裡的 feel like 用法一模一樣，這裡是表示「聽起來」的感覺。如果一定要嚴加區別，就是英美人士用本句型時，sound 多半就用在句首，也就是省略前面的主詞 That、It 之類。不過要注意，省略主詞時，sound 還是要加 s，表示省略第三人稱單數主詞，不影響動詞形式。

句型 連結站

## That sounds like a good idea.

那聽起來好像是個好主意。

## Sounds like you had a good time.

聽起來你好像玩得很愉快。

## It sounds like you don't like her.

那聽起來，你好像不喜歡她。

**A** We're going to the zoo tomorrow.

**B** That **sounds like** fun.

**A** I think it will be.
Would you like to join us?

**B** I'd love to.

A 我們明天要去動物園。

B 聽起來，好像很好玩的樣子。

A 我想會很好玩的。
你要不要和我們一起去？

B 我喜歡和你們一起去。

☑ sound
[saʊnd]
v. 聽起來

☑ zoo
[zu]
動物園

☑ have a good time
玩得很愉快

☑ join
[dʒɔɪn]
加入

# ~ really neat

…真的很好

**句型 模擬站**

## It was **really neat**.

那真的很好。

**句型解析站**

really neat 是純美語。

　　neat 原意是「井然有序」，但在這裡，與有序無序毫無關連。美語中，只要我喜歡，有什麼不neat? 嬉皮的衣服、龐克族的頭髮、男人的耳洞都可以 really neat 啦！

**句型 連結站**

## I like your speech. It was really neat.

我喜歡你的演講，它真的很好。

## The place is neat.

這個地方真的很好。

## Your dress is neat. I like it.

你的衣服真的很好。我喜歡。

**A** Have you seen that new book-store and coffee shop?

**B** No, but I heard about it.
The coffee shop is inside the bookstore.

**A** Yes, I was there yesterday.
It was **really neat**.

**B** I'll have to go soon.

A 你看過那家新的書店和咖啡館了嗎？

B 不，不過，我聽說了。
咖啡館就在書店裡面。

A 是的，我昨天去了。
那個地方真的很好。

B 那我要趕快去才行。

☑ neat
[nit]
很棒；很舒服；
很好

☑ speech
[spitʃ]
演講

☑ dress
[drɛs]
洋裝

☑ bookstore
[ˈbuk͵stor]
書店

☑ shop
[ʃɑp]
店

☑ inside
[ˈɪnˈsaɪd]
在裡面

# How do you like it?

你還喜歡嗎?

## 句型 模擬站

## How do you like it?
你還喜歡嗎?

### 句型解析站

How的原意是「如何」,但是 How do you ~? 的句型也可以是詢問對方某種行為的「程度」,不一定是詢問「方法」。下列句型連結站中,兩種用法都有,請注意其不同之處。

### 句型 連結站

How do you take it?
這件事,你的反應如何?

How do you make it?
你是怎麼做到的?

How do you speak English without an accent?
怎樣說英語才能不帶一點外國腔?

**A** I heard you got a new job.

**B** Yes, I'm doing accounting for a real estate developer.

**A** How do you like it?

**B** So far, I'm really enjoying it.

A 我聽說你換了一個新工作。

B 是的，我現在幫一家不動產建築商做會計。

A 你還喜歡嗎？

B 到目前為止，我還真的很喜歡。

☑ accent
['æksɛnt]
腔調

☑ accounting
[ə'kauntɪŋ]
會計

☑ real estate
['rɪəl ə'stet]
房地產

☑ developer
[dɪ'vɛləpə]
開發商

☑ so far
到目前為止

# 015

## too ~ to ~

### 太…所以不能…

MP3-16

## It's **too** cold **to** eat.
東西太冷，不能吃。

### 句型解析站

　　這個 too ~ to 的句型，從國中到托福測驗，沒有不考的，原因是它太常用了。問題是，在會話上你可以運用自如嗎？

　　熟練應用本句型的秘訣，在於忘掉「太…所以不能」等於too ~ to，而要按字面的含意「太…了，假如要…的話」來運用，例如「太暗所以照片拍不起來。」，要想成「太暗了」too dark，「要拍照片的話」to take a picture，全句就是It's too dark to take a picture.。

### 句型 連結站

## It's too hot to play basketball.
天氣太熱，不能打籃球。

## It's too dark to see clearly.
太暗了，看不清楚。

I am too tired to speak.
我累得說不出話來。

☑ basketball
　['bæskɪt,bɔl]
　籃球

☑ dark
　[dɑrk]
　暗的

**會話　轉播站**

A　Sorry I'm late.
　Is that my dinner?

B　Yes, but I think it's **too** cold **to** eat.

A　That's okay.
　I'll warm it up in the microwave.

B　Here, I'll get it for you.

☑ clearly
　['klɪrlɪ]
　清楚地

☑ tired
　[taɪrd]
　疲倦的

☑ microwave
　['maɪkrə,wev]
　微波爐

A　對不起，我來晚了。
　那是我的晚餐嗎？

B　是的，不過我看東西冷了，不能吃。

A　還好。
　我把它擺到微波爐裏熱一下。

B　來吧，我來幫你做。

MP3-17

# I didn't know ~

我不曉得…

**I didn't know** you did that kind of writing.

我不曉得你在寫那種文章。

### 句型解析站

　　一般人只知道 I didn't know. 我不知道。這句話單獨使用,而不知它的後面可以接你所不知道的那件事。在對話中,語意愈清楚愈好,所以有時可以簡單,有時要不厭其煩。這裡屬於後者。

### 句型 連結站

I didn't know you drew it with the computer.

我不知道你是用電腦畫出來的圖。

I didn't know she worked for ABC company.

我不知道她在ABC公司上班。

I didn't know he was the richest person in the world.
我不知道他是全世界最有錢的人。

☑ kind
[kaɪnd]
種類

## 會話 轉播站

**A** Did you see the article I wrote for the newsletter?

----------

**B** Yes, it was very good.
**I didn't know** you did that kind of writing.

----------

**A** Actually, that was the first time I've written a news story.
Usually I stick with fiction.

----------

**B** Well, I think you do both quite well.

☑ writing
['raɪtɪŋ]
寫作

☑ drew
[dru]
畫（draw的過去式）

☑ article
['ɑrtɪkl]
文章

☑ stick
[stɪk]
堅持於

☑ fiction
['fɪkʃən]
小說

☑ quite
[kwaɪt]
相當地

A 你有沒有看到我替新聞通訊寫的文章？

B 有啊，寫得非常好。
我不知道你會寫那種文章。

A 事實上，這是我第一次寫新聞報導。
通常我都是專門寫小說。

B 是嗎，我想你兩樣都寫得很好。

43

# getting ~ for ~

## 獲得…以做為…

**句型 模擬站**

Mary is **getting** a new car **for** graduation.

瑪麗獲得一部新車做為畢業禮物。

**句型解析站**

　　本句型使用在「因為某種事件或場合而獲得某種東西」。

　　get 原意是「取得」，主要意義在「得到」而不論「來源」，所以可能是自行購買，或別人贈送。for 之後的部分是指場合而言，中的例子是因為畢業而得到新車，所以用 for graduation 。若不特別說明場合的話，for 的部分就可不提。

**句型 連結站**

John is getting a new TV set.

約翰獲得一台新的電視。

I'm getting a new computer for birthday present.

我得到一部新電腦，做為我的生日禮物。

Guess what, I am getting a new job.
猜猜看，我已經獲得一個新工作。

☑ graduation
[ˌɡrædʒʊˈeʃən]
畢業

**A** Mary is **getting** a new car **for** graduation.

**B** Wow! Who's buying it?

**A** I think her grandparents are buying it.

**B** That's great. She really deserves it.

☑ present
[ˈprɛznt]
禮物

☑ guess
[ɡɛs]
猜想

☑ deserve
[dɪˈzɝv]
值得受獎賞

A 瑪麗得到一部新車，做為她的畢業禮物。

B 哇！是誰幫她買的？

A 我想是她的祖父母幫她買的吧。

B 那真好。其實是她應得的。

# Where did you ~?

你從那裡…呢？

**句型 模擬站**

## Where did you learn to play bridge?
你從哪裡學會打橋牌的呢？

**句型解析站**

人與人之間的對話，大都是一問一答，所以問句的形式要會熟練運用。本句是問別人「來源」，英語是Where 哪裡。注意中文裡「來源」可以是地點，也可以是人，但英語的 Where 是指地點而言，假如來源不是一個地點，那你就要費一番口舌，一面解釋來源，一面詳細說明並非來自一個地點，像會話轉播站裡的例子就是這種情形。

**句型 連結站**

Where did you learn to type?
你在哪裡學會打字？

Where did you go to college?
你上哪一間大學？

Where did you learn to speak English?
你從哪裡學會說英語的呢？

**A** **Where did you** learn to play bridge?

**B** My parents played when I was a child.
When I was old enough to learn, they taught me.

**A** I would really like to learn how.

**B** I can teach you if you would like.

☑ bridge
[brɪdʒ]
橋牌

☑ taught
[tɔt]
教（teach的過去式）

☑ type
[taɪp]
打字

☑ college
[ˈkɑlɪdʒ]
大學

☑ learn
[lɝn]
學習

A 你從哪裡學會打橋牌的呢？

B 當我還是小孩子時，我父母常玩。
當我比較大可以學的時候，他們就教我。

A 我也很喜歡學打橋牌。

B 如果你喜歡的話，我可以教你呀。

# *019*

# Would you like to ~?

你想要…嗎?

## 句型 模擬站

## Would you like to try it?

你要不要試一下?

### 句型解析站

　　這個句型最好就是把前四個字 Would you like to背起來,當詢問對方是否有意做什麼事時,就先拋出這四個英文字,再接「做該事」的動作就行。例如問對方是否有意吃蛋糕 (have a piece of cake),就先說 Would you like to 再接have a piece of cake ,成為 Would you like to have a piece of cake? 就對了。

### 句型 連結站

Would you like to go to the seminar?
你要不要去參加研討會?

Would you like to take the computer course?
你要不要選這門電腦課?

Would you like to go to a movie?
你要不要去看電影?

**A** That looks interesting.
What are you doing?

**B** It's called finger weaving.

**A** It looks hard.

**B** It isn't.
**Would you like to try it?**

---

A 那看起來真的很有趣。
你在做什麼？

B 這叫做手指編織。

A 看起來很困難。

B 不困難的。
你要不要試一下？

---

☑ try
[traɪ]
嘗試

☑ seminar
['sɛmə,nɑr]
研討會

☑ course
[kors]
課程

☑ finger
['fɪŋgɚ]
手指頭

☑ weaving
['wivɪŋ]
編織

# I tried ~

## 我試過…

### 句型 模擬站

**I tried** jogging for a while, but I can't stand the heat in the summer.

有一陣子我試過慢跑,不過我受不了夏天的熱氣。

### 句型解析站

　　本句型之所以常用,是有時難免要找藉口為自己解釋。英語句型 I tried ,先用過去式表示「我試過」,再用 but 帶出藉口來,就可告訴對方,不是我懶或笨,而是有其他原因的。注意 tried 後面要用動名詞,就是動詞本身的字後面要加 ing。

### 句型 連結站

I tried teaching him for a while, but he didn't want to learn.

有一陣子我試著教他,可是他不想學。

I tried reading the book, but I can't stand its writing style.

我試過讀這本書,但是它的寫作風格我不能忍受。

**I tried losing weight, but nothing worked.**

我試著減肥，但是每樣都無效。

會話 轉播站

**A** These tomatoes are wonderful.

**B** Thanks. I grew them in the garden.

**A** **I tried** gardening for a while, but I can't stand the heat in the summer.

**B** It does get hot.
I get up at 5:00 to go out before it gets hot.

A 這些蕃茄非常好。

B 謝謝你。我是在自己的花園種的。

A 有一陣子我也試著種菜、種花，不過我忍受不了夏天的熱氣。

B 天氣真的是很熱。
我都是五點起床，天氣開始變熱以前出去弄的。

單字 片語加油站

☑ style
[staɪl]
文體；寫作風格

☑ weight
[wet]
體重

☑ tomato
[tə'meto]
蕃茄

☑ grew
[gru]
種植（grow的過去式）

☑ garden
['gɑrdn̩]
v. 種花；n. 花圃

☑ stand
[stænd]
忍受

☑ heat
[hit]
熱氣

☑ get up
起床

# *021* What are you doing?
### 你有什麼活動？

**句型 模擬站**

## What are you doing this weekend?
這個週末你有什麼活動？

**句型解析站**

　　這個句型如果單獨使用，What are you doing? 可以解釋成「你正在做什麼？」或「你幹啥？」，但若有接「時間」的話，那就是「你要~」或「你有~」的意思，反倒沒有「正在」現在進行式的含意了。

　　至於 are you 後面的動詞不一定要接 doing（做），而可以更明確一點用 planning（計劃）或 going（去）一類的其他動詞。

**句型 連結站**

What are you planning on the vacation?
你的假期打算做什麼？

Where are you going this summer?
今年夏天你要去哪裡？

When are you going to get married?
你準備幾時結婚？

**A** **What are you doing** this week-end?

**B** A bunch of us are going to the lake to ski.
Would you like to join us?

**A** That sounds like it might be fun.
I can't go the whole weekend,
but maybe Saturday.

**B** Drive up whenever you can.
You know where the lake house is, don't you?

A 你這個週末有什麼活動？

B 我們有一群人要去湖上划水。
你要不要一起來？

A 聽起來好像很有趣的樣子。
我不能整個週末都去，不過也許禮拜六還可以。

B 你可以的話，就開車過來吧。
你知道湖邊小屋在哪裡，不是嗎？

☑ vacation
[ve'keʃən]
假期

☑ a bunch of
許多

☑ ski
[ski]
滑雪

☑ join
[dʒɔɪn]
加入

☑ whole
[hol]
全部的

☑ Saturday
['sætɚde]
星期六

☑ drive
[draɪv]
開車

☑ lake
[lek]
湖

# 022

## ~ birthday is ~

生日是在…

### 句型 模擬站

Tom's **birthday is** this week.
湯姆的生日就在這個星期。

### 句型解析站

　　本句型是社交常用句型，表面上很簡單，birthday 的前面用人的所有格，表示某人的生日，而 is 的後面用時間，表示生日是在某個時候。但請注意，很多人在 is 和時間之間多用了不該用的 at, in, on 之類的介系詞，下回交朋友，互相問生日時，千萬別出錯了！

### 句型 連結站

The graduation ceremony is this week.
畢業典禮就在這個星期。

The 25th anniversary is next week.
25週年紀念日就在下個星期。

The Fourth of July is next Saturday.
國慶7月4日是在下個禮拜六。

**A** There is so much going on this week.

**B** I know.
Mary's **birthday is** this week.
What are you getting her?

**A** I don't know yet.
What about you?

**B** I haven't gotten to the store yet, either.
Do you want to go together later today?

☑ birthday
['bɝθ,de]
生日

☑ ceremony
['sɛrə,monɪ]
典禮

☑ anniversary
[,ænə'vɝsərɪ]
週年紀念

☑ together
[tə'gɛðɚ]
一起

A 這個禮拜事情這麼多。

B 我知道。
瑪麗的生日就在這個禮拜。
你要送她什麼東西？

A 我還不知道。
你呢？

B 我也還沒有到店裡去看。
今天稍後你要不要跟我一起去？

# 023

# Did you know ~?
你知道…嗎？

**句型 模擬站**

**Did you know Mr. Wang is now the school principal?**
你知道王老師，現在已經是學校的校長了嗎？

**句型解析站**

有些事我們想問對方是不是知道，用Did you know 這個句型去問。

**句型 連結站**

Did you know Mr. Lin is now the president of Gold Star Company?
你知道林先生現在是金星公司的總經理了嗎？

Did you know Ms. Lin is now holding the meeting?
你知道林小姐現在正在主持會議嗎？

Did you know John is now a college student?
你知道約翰現在已經是大學生了嗎？

**A** How are things going at your kids' school this year?

**B** They are great.
**Did you know** Mr. Wang is now the school principal?

**A** No, I didn't!
That is wonderful news.

**B** Yes, that is why things are going so well.

☑ principal
['prɪnsəpl]
校長

☑ hold
[hold]
主持

☑ president
['prɛzədənt]
總裁

☑ wonderful
['wʌndɚfəl]
很棒的

☑ news
[njuz]
消息

A 你小孩的學校今年怎麼樣啊？

B 他們都很好。
你知道王老師，現在已經是學校的校長嗎？

A 不，我不曉得！
真是個大好的消息。

B 是啊，所有的事情才會進行的那麼順利。

## 024

# was + p.p.
被別人…

## John **was fired**.
約翰被開除了。

### 句型解析站

　　英文句型裏有一種叫被動式，它的用法是 be 動詞加上過去分詞，若是這件事是過去發生的事，要用過去式被動，也就是 was 或 were 加上過去分詞。

### 句型 連結站

Mary was paid $1500 to do the job.
瑪麗做這差事，獲得1500美元。

I was given two hours to make my decision.
我要在兩個鐘頭內做決定。

He was given 3 days to clean up the mess.
他被限在三天之內，把所有髒亂清除乾淨。

**A** John **was fired** from his job yesterday.

**B** That's terrible!
How is he taking it?

**A** Fairly well actually.
There was a lot of negative stuff going on.
I think he's glad to be out of there.

**B** I hope so.
I expect he'll find a new position quickly.

☑ fire
[faɪr]
開除

☑ paid
[ped]
付錢（pay的過去分詞）

☑ clean up
整理乾淨

☑ mess
[mɛs]
髒亂

☑ terrible
['tɛrəbl̩]
可怕的

☑ negative
['nɛɡətɪv]
負面的

☑ stuff
[stʌf]
東西；成分

☑ position
[pə'zɪʃən]
職位

☑ quickly
['kwɪklɪ]
很快地

A 約翰昨天被開除了。

B 那真是糟糕。
這件事，他的反應如何？

A 事實上，還很好。
他們公司現在有太多負面成份了。
我想他也很高興離開那個地方。

B 但願如此。
我希望他很快就可以找到一個新的工作。

# *025*

# Will ~?
## 會不會…呢？

MP3-26

**句型** **模擬站**

## **Will** his parents be home**?**
他父母會不會在家呢？

**句型解析站**

> 問某人會不會怎麼樣呢？用「Will + 某人」這個句型。

**句型** **連結站**

Will he be in the office?
他會不會在辦公室呢？

Will you be late for work?
你上班會不會遲到呢？

Will she be home?
她會不會在家呢？

**A** Mom, may I go over to David's house?

**B** What are you planning on doing?

**A** Working on our homework.

**B** **Will** his parents be home?

**A** No, but his grandparents are there.

**B** Okay, but be home before six for dinner.

☑ weekend
['wik'ɛnd]
週末

☑ library
['laɪˌbrɛrɪ]
圖書館

☑ parent
['pɛrənt]
父母親

☑ go over to someplace
到某地方去

A 媽，我可以到大衛家嗎？

B 你們打算做什麼事？

A 做我們的功課。

B 他的父母會不會在家？

A 不在，不過他的祖父母會在。

B 好吧，但是在六點以前要回家吃晚飯。

MP3-27

# *026* Can you ~?

能請你…嗎？

句型 模擬站

## Can you cover for me on Friday?

星期五能不能請你幫我代班？

### 句型解析站

請人幫你做某事，可以用 Can you ~, Could you ~ 或 Would you ~ 這幾種用法。

### 句型 連結站

Can you type the paper for me?
能不能請你幫我打這篇報告？

Can you get a cup of coffee for me?
能不能請你幫我倒杯咖啡？

Can you pass the salt, please?
能不能請你把鹽遞給我？

**A** What a week!
David's sister is getting married this weekend.

**B** Aren't you scheduled to be on call?

**A** Yes, but I switched with Mary.
So she's covering for me on Saturday.
**Can you** cover for me on Friday?

**B** I think so, but let me check my schedule.

A 這個星期真是的！
大衛的姊姊這個週末要結婚。

B 這個週末，你不是要隨時待命的嗎？

A 是呀，不過我和瑪麗調班。
所以禮拜六她幫我代班。
禮拜五可不可以請你代班？

B 我想可以吧，不過先讓我查一下我的行程表。

☑ cover for ~
替～代班

☑ paper
['pepɚ]
報告

☑ pass
[pæs]
遞過來

☑ salt
[sɔlt]
鹽

☑ get married
結婚

☑ on call
隨時待命

☑ switch
[swɪtʃ]
交換

☑ check
[tʃɛk]
查一查

☑ schedule
['skɛdʒʊl]
v. 排訂時間；
n. 時間表

# It's supposed to ~

那應當是…

## 句型 模擬站

**It's supposed to** be good.

那應當是相當好的。

## 句型解析站

若你認為某人或某件事應該是怎麼樣時,記住用 be supposed to 這個片語。其句型是主詞 + be supposed to + 原形動詞。這個句型裏的主詞就是你認為應該會怎麼樣的某人或某件事。

## 句型 連結站

The meeting is supposed to be over.

會議應當是結束了。

He is supposed to arrive any time now.

他應當隨時都會抵達。

The show is supposed to be good.

這場表演應當是相當好的。

**A** There's a new film coming out this Friday.
Do you want to go see it?

**B** I guess so.
What's it about?

**A** Oh, it's a love story set in post World War II California.

**B** I've heard about it.
**It's supposed to** be good.

A 這個星期五,有一部新片要上演。
你要不要去看?

B 應該會吧。
演什麼呢?

A 喔,那是一個愛情故事,發生在二次世界大戰後的加州。

B 我聽說過了。
那應當是一部相當好的片子。

☑ suppose
[sə'poz]
應當

☑ over
['ovɚ]
結束

☑ arrive
[ə'raɪv]
到達

☑ film
[fɪlm]
影片

☑ post
[post]
在~之後

☑ set
[sɛt]
背景被設在~
(過去分詞)

☑ post World War II
在第二次世界大戰之後

# 028

## I'll have to ~

我必須…

MP3-29

句型 模擬站

**I'll have to** check my schedule.

我必須查一下我的行程表。

### 句型解析站

　　have to 這個片語是「必須」的意思，用在 I'll have to 這個句型裏，表示這件必須做的事不是現在必須要做，而是指未來必須要做。當然這未來不一定是很久以後，它可以是等一會兒，或是明天，或是下星期都可以。

句型 連結站

I'll have to ask my boss first.

我必須先問一下我的老板。

I'll have to turn it in tomorrow.

我必須明天交上去。

I'll have to tell you a secret.

我必須告訴你一個秘密。

**A** Can you baby-sit for me Thursday evening?

**B** I think so, but **I'll have to** check my schedule.

**A** That's fine.  Do you want to call me later?

**B** Yes, I'll let you know as soon as I get home.

☑ boss
[bɔs]
上司，老闆

☑ turn in
繳交

☑ secret
['sikrɪt]
秘密

☑ baby-sit
['bæbɪ'sɪt]
幫忙看顧小孩

A 你星期四晚上，能不能幫我看小孩？

B 我想可以吧，不過我得先查一下我的行程表。

A 好吧。你稍後要不要給我一通電話？

B 好，我一到家，一定儘快通知你。

# 029

## be scheduled to ~

排定日期…

MP3-30

**I'm scheduled to** have surgery on Monday.

我排在星期一動手術。

### 句型解析站

日程已經排好了要去做某件事，注意用 be scheduled to這個片語，be這個字隨主詞以及時間而改變，若是排好要去做，用 am, are, is。若是指某件事原本排定，用 was 和were。

### 句型 連結站

I'm scheduled to attend the training camp next Tuesday.
我排在下星期二，參加訓練營。

We're scheduled to meet the reporter this afternoon.
我們排定在今天下午跟記者見面。

The meeting was scheduled for two hours, but it is not over yet.

會議是排定二個小時，不過到現在還沒有結束。

**會話** **轉播站**

**A** How is your hand doing?

--------------------------------------------

**B** Not very well.
The doctor does not think it's doing well.
She wants to do a bone graft.

--------------------------------------------

**A** Yucca! That sounds painful.
When are they going to do it?

--------------------------------------------

**B** **I'm scheduled to** have surgery on Monday.

--------------------------------------------

A 你的手現在情況怎樣？

B 不怎麼好。
醫生認為我的手的情況不好。
她要做一個接骨手術。

A 哎呀！聽起來會很痛的樣子。
他們準備什麼時候做？

B 我已經排定禮拜一動手術。

☑ schedule
['skɛdʒʊl]
排定時間

☑ surgery
['sɝdʒərɪ]
手術

☑ attend
[ə'tɛnd]
參加

☑ training
['trenɪŋ]
訓練

☑ camp
[kæmp]
營地

☑ reporter
[rɪ'portɚ]
記者

☑ bone graft
[bon græft]
接骨手術

☑ painful
['penfəl]
痛的

# 030

# It really depends on ~

那全視…情況而定。

**句型 模擬站**

**It really depends** on what kind of seasonings you use.

那全視你用的是什麼樣的調味料而定。

**句型解析站**

　　It really depends on ~ 表示「視什麼樣的情況來決定」。這句話後面接由 what, where, who, whether 或 how 等疑問詞帶出來的句子。

**句型 連結站**

It really depends on what kind of media you use.

那純粹要看你用的是什麼樣的媒體。

It really depends on whether you understand it or not.

那全視你是否理解而定。

It really depends on who makes the decision.

那完全要看是誰做的決定而定。

A This soup is wonderful.
What makes it so good?

--------------------------------------

B **It really depends on** what kind of seasonings you use.

--------------------------------------

A What do you mean?

--------------------------------------

B I always try to use pork ribs for soup.
The food simply seasons better.

--------------------------------------

A 這個湯太棒了。
是什麼讓它這麼好喝呢？

B 那全要看你用的是什麼調味料。

A 你是什麼意思呢？

B 我總是試著用豬排骨熬湯。
這樣食物比較會入味。

☑ depend
[dɪ'pɛnd]
依賴

☑ kind
[kaɪnd]
種類

☑ seasoning
['siznɪŋ]
調味料

☑ media
['midɪə]
媒體

☑ whether
['hwɛðɚ]
是否

☑ decision
[dɪ'sɪʒən]
決定

☑ soup
[sup]
湯

☑ pork
[pork]
豬肉

☑ rib
[rɪb]
肋骨

☑ pork rib soup
高湯

☑ season
['sizn̩]
調味

71

# 031

## ended up ~

最終是…

MP3-32

句型 模擬站

**We ended up** in New York instead of California.

我們最終是在紐約,而不是在加州。

---

### 句型解析站

end up 這個片語,是用在向別人述說,你最終是做了某件事,或是你最終是得了什麼結果,或是你最終是到某個地方。因為是向別人述說過去的一件事,所以要用過去式 詞ended up。

---

句型 連結站

I ended up having to pay for everyone's dinner.

我最後必須為大家付晚餐的錢。

After swimming at night, we all ended up with colds.

在晚上游泳之後,我們結果都得了感冒。

We were late for the show, and ended up watching it on a big screen.
我們趕不上這一場表演，最後必須要在大銀幕觀賞。

☑ A instead of B
是A而不是B

☑ cold
[kold]
感冒

☑ screen
[skrin]
銀幕

☑ airplane
['ɛr,plen]
飛機

☑ wrong
[rɔŋ]
錯誤的

☑ by mistake
弄錯

**會話 轉播站**

**A** How was your trip this weekend?

**B** Horrible. We took the wrong airplane by mistake.

**A** You're kidding!
What happened?

**B** We **ended up** in New York instead of California.

A 你們這個週末的旅遊如何？

B 太糟糕了。我們搭錯了飛機。

A 你在開什麼玩笑！
怎麼搞的？

B 我們最終到了紐約，而不是加州。

73

# 032

## You are right about ~

你對…的看法是正確的。

**句型 模擬站**

## You are right about the cost.

你對成本的看法是正確的。

### 句型解析站

談話中，某人提到一個論點，你很同意對方的看法，可以用 You are right about 這件事。如果這個論點是對方以前提出的，你告訴對方，他以前提到對某件事的看法很正確，要用 You were right about 那件事。注意句中 are 和 were的用法。

**句型 連結站**

You are right about the stock market.
你對股票市場的看法是對的。

He is right about the pollution.
他對污染的看法是對的。

You were right about the outcome of the election.
你對選舉結果的看法是對的。

**A** Mary, this is a wonderful article.

**B** Do you think so?
I wasn't sure about that last paragraph.

**A** Overall, it is great.
But **you are right about** the last paragraph.
It isn't very clear.

☑ wonderful
['wʌndɚfəl]
很棒的

☑ article
['ɑrtɪk!]
文章

☑ content
['kɑntɛnt]
內容

☑ paragraph
['pærə,græf]
段落

A 瑪麗,這篇文章非常好。

B 你真的這麼認為嗎?
我認為最後一段不太好。

A 總的來說,整篇文章是很好。
不過,你對最後一段的看法是對的。
它寫得不是很清楚。

# 033

## It's not just ~, though.

### 不過，那不僅是…而已。

MP3-34

**句型 模擬站**

**It's not just** the noise, **though**.

不過，那不只是噪音而已。

---

**句型解析站**

在談話中，你們在研究一個問題的原因，有人提出一個原因，你認為那個原因只是其中的一個，但不僅僅是那個原因而已，記住這個句型 It's not just 這個原因，though 。

---

**句型 連結站**

It's not just his English, though.
不過，那不只是他的英語而已。

It's not just the cost, though.
不過，那不僅是成本的問題而已。

It's not just a matter of time, though.
不過，那不僅是時間的問題而已。

**A** I have a horrible headache.

**B** From all the noise?

**A** Yes. **It's not just** the noise, **though**.
The heat is making it worse, too.

**B** Why don't you go lie down for a while?
I'll handle things here.

---

A 我的頭痛得厲害。

B 是因為這些噪音嗎？

A 是的。不過，那不僅是噪音而已。
熱氣使我的頭，痛得更厲害。

B 你為什麼不去躺一會兒呢？
我會處理這裡的事情。

☑ though
　[ðo]
　然而；不過

☑ noise
　[nɔɪz]
　噪音

☑ matter
　['mætɚ]
　問題

☑ horrible
　['hɔrəbl̩]
　可怕的

☑ headache
　['hɛdˌek]
　頭痛

☑ worse
　[wɝs]
　更糟（bad的比較級）

☑ lie down
　躺下

☑ handle
　['hændl̩]
　處理

☑ heat
　[hit]
　熱

## 034

MP3-35

# Is that why ~?

## 就是這個緣故才導致…嗎？

句型 模擬站

**Is that why they are absent from school?**

就是這個緣故才導致他們缺席嗎？

句型解析站

　　有人告訴你一件事，你認為這件事可能就是導致另一個結果的原因，你可以用這個句型 Is that why 接你認為所導致的結果，如例句中的 they are absent from school （他們沒去上學）。

句型 連結站

Is that why you are late for work?
就是這個緣故，你才上班遲到嗎？

Is that why you didn't buy it?
就是這個緣故，你才沒有買嗎？

Is that why you don't want to go home?
就是這個緣故，你才不想回家的嗎？

**A** The Smiths went to their grand-parents' house this week.

**B** Really? **Is that why** they are absent from school?

**A** Yes. Their grandmother is very sick.

**B** I hope she is doing better.

☑ absent
　['æbsn̩t]
　缺席的

☑ grandparent
　['grænd‚pɛrənt]
　祖父母

☑ sick
　[sɪk]
　生病的

A 史密斯一家人，這個禮拜去探望他們的祖父母。

B 真的嗎？就是這個緣故，他們才缺席，沒有上學嗎？

A 是的。他們的祖母病得很厲害。

B 我希望她現在好一點。

## 035

# I guess ~

我猜想…

MP3-36

### 句型 模擬站

**I guess** I expected more drama.

我猜想，我是期待更富有戲劇性一點。

#### 句型解析站

　　談話時，有些情況是有點你假設或你認為應該是這樣時，可以在你要說的情況之前，加 I guess。

### 句型 連結站

I guess I expected more input from the others.

我猜想，我是期待從他人那裡得到更多的意見。

I guess I expected more feedback from my customers.

我希望我能從我的顧客那裡，得到更多回饋的意見。

I guess I expected 100% of hard work from my employees.

我猜想我希望我的雇員，能百之百地努力工作。

**A** How was your first day in court?

**B** It was real different.
Not at all what I expected.

**A** What do you mean?

**B** **I guess** I expected more drama,
like on TV.
It was actually rather boring.

---

A 你第一天上法庭如何？

B 一切都很不同。
絲毫都不是我預期的。

A 你這話，是什麼意思呢？

B 我想我希望更富戲劇性一點，就像是在電視上
看到的。
不過，事實上是很無聊的。

☑ expect
[ɪkˈspɛkt]
期待

☑ drama
[ˈdrɑmə]
戲劇

☑ input
[ˈɪnpʊt]
提供意見；看法

☑ feedback
[ˈfidbæk]
反應的意見

☑ court
[kɔrt]
法院；法庭

☑ actually
[ˈæktʃʊəlɪ]
實際上

☑ rather
[ˈræðɚ]
相當地

☑ boring
[ˈborɪŋ]
無聊的；乏味的

# 036

# What makes you ~?

什麼事讓你…呢？

MP3-37

## What makes you think that?

什麼事你這樣想呢？

### 句型解析站

What makes you 這個句型是用來問對方「什麼事會讓你…？」，注意 What makes you 句中的 make 是使役動詞，後面要接原形動詞。

### 句型 連結站

## What makes you change your mind?

什麼事讓你改變主意呢？

## What makes you make the progress?

什麼事讓你這樣進步呢？

## What makes you feel so bad?

什麼事讓你心情這樣壞呢？

**A** I'm afraid John is going to be fired if he isn't careful.

**B** What makes you think that?

**A** His boss is watching John's every move.

**B** You're right.
It's like he's waiting for John to screw up.

☑ mind
[maɪnd]
心意

☑ progress
[ˈprɑgrɛs]
進步

☑ move
[muv]
舉動

☑ screw up
[ˈskru ˈʌp]
出差錯

A 我恐怕約翰不小心的話，會被開除。

B 什麼事讓你這樣想呢？

A 他的老闆，都在注意約翰的每一個舉動。

B 你是對的。

就好像他的老闆，在等著他出差錯似的。

# 037

## I know what ~

我知道…是什麼。

MP3-38

## I know what you mean.
我知道你的意思是什麼。

### 句型解析站

I know 我知道後面所接的句子做 I know 的受詞，所以雖有疑問副詞 what, where, when ，卻不是用疑問句的句型，而是用肯定句的句型，例如用 what you mean，而不是 what do you mean。用 Where the TV station is，而不是 Where is the TV station。

### 句型 連結站

I know what you like.
我知道，你喜歡的是什麼。

I know where the TV station is.
我知道電視台在什麼地方。

I know when he will be back.
我知道，他幾時會回來。

**A** John is driving me nuts.
If he takes a nap, he is up until eleven or twelve at night.
But if he doesn't, he's so cranky.

**B** **I know what** you mean.
My Mary is doing the same thing.

**A** I hope it would get better soon.

**B** It should.

☑ station
['steʃən]
電視台

☑ nuts
[nʌts]
發瘋

☑ cranky
['kræŋkɪ]
易發脾氣的

☑ take a nap
睡午覺

A 約翰使我快要發瘋了。
如果他睡了午覺,他晚上就要搞到11、12點。
不過,如果他不睡午覺,他就處處不對勁。

B 我知道你的意思。
我家瑪麗,也是一樣的問題。

A 我希望情況會趕快好轉。

B 應該會的。

## 038

MP3-39

# Can you imagine ~?

你能想像…嗎?

句型 模擬站

**Can you imagine** being able to sail around the world?

你能夠想像,坐船環繞世界嗎?

### 句型解析站

這個句型要注意 imagine 後面要接動名詞 Ving。Can you imagine + 做某件事,就是「你能想像做這件事的滋味嗎?」

句型 連結站

Can you imagine watching a Broadway show in New York?

你能夠想像,在紐約看一場百老匯表演嗎?

Can you imagine walking on the moon?

你能想像在月球漫步嗎?

Can you imagine going out with her?

你能想像跟她出去約會的滋味嗎?

**A** I am so envious of John and Mary.
Can you imagine being able to sail around the world?

----

**B** I would love to be able to some day.
But not every one is able to take a three month leave like that.

----

**A** I'm going to put it on my wish lists.

----

**B** Me too.

----

☑ sail
　[sel]
　坐帆船

☑ Broadway
　['brɔd,we]
　百老匯

☑ imagine
　[ɪ'mædʒɪn]
　想像

☑ envious
　['ɛnvɪəs]
　嫉妒的

☑ take ~ leave
　請（幾天）的假

A 我非常羨慕約翰和瑪麗。
　你能想像，搭船環繞世界嗎？

B 我希望有一天也能這樣做。
　不過，並不是每一個人都可以像他們一樣，請三個月的假。

A 我要把這一件事，放在心願表上面。

B 我也要。

## 039

# enjoy ~

## 很喜歡…

MP3-40

## He **enjoys** being outdoors.

他很喜歡在戶外。

### 句型解析站

　　enjoy 這個字是「很喜歡」的意思，後面要接動名名詞Ving，例如： being、lying 和 riding 等。

### 句型 連結站

I enjoy lying in the sun.
我很喜歡躺在陽光下。

We enjoy riding the bike in the park.
我們很喜歡在公園裡騎腳踏車。

I enjoy working with you very much.
我很喜歡和你一起工作。

**A** Jim and I are going camping and rock climbing this weekend.

**B** Wow! Is this the first time for you to do that?

**A** Yes, but Jim goes all the time. He **enjoys** being outdoors.

**B** That doesn't surprise me.

---

A 吉姆和我這個週末要一起露營並且攀岩。

B 哇！這是你第一次這樣做嗎？

A 是的，不過吉姆經常去。
他喜歡在戶外。

B 那我不感到驚訝。

☑ enjoy
[ɪnˈdʒɔɪ]
很喜歡

☑ lying
[ˈlaɪɪŋ]
躺著（lie的動名詞）

☑ rock
[rɑk]
岩石

☑ climb
[klaɪm]
攀登、爬（climbing 名詞）

☑ outdoors
[ˈaʊtˈdorz]
在戶外

☑ riding
[ˈraɪdɪŋ]
騎（腳踏車）（ride的動名詞）

# You look ~

你看起來…

## 句型 模擬站

**You look** angry.

你看起來很生氣。

### 句型解析站

look （看起來）是個連綴動詞，後面要接形容詞，如例句中的 angry, worried, sad 和 down。

## 句型 連結站

You look worried.

你看起來很憂慮。

You look sad.

你看起來，心情很悲傷。

He looks down.

他看起來，情緒很壞。

**A** What's wrong?
**You look** angry.

---

**B** I am.
I worked hard on a presentation and then Robert stole the credit.

---

**A** You mean he took credit for your work?

---

**B** Yes! He acted like all I did was type it.

---

☑ down
[daʊn]
精神沮喪

☑ stole
[stol]
偷取（steal的過去式）

☑ credit
[ˈkrɛdɪt]
功勞

☑ type
[taɪp]
打字

A 出了什麼事了？
你看起來很生氣。

B 我是很生氣。
我很努力準備發表會，然後羅伯把所有的功勞都搶走了。

A 你的意思是，他搶走了你工作的功勞？

B 是的！他表現的好像我所做的只是打字而已。

# 041

## I heard ~

我聽說…

MP3-42

**I heard** he was fired.

我聽說他被開除了。

### 句型解析站

當你要說你聽說的某個消息時，要用 hear 的過去式heard，I heard（我聽說）後面接 that，由 that 帶出你聽說的句子，但 that 可以省略掉。

### 句型 連結站

I heard Mary is going to leave the company.

我聽說瑪麗就要離開這個公司。

Did you hear that our company is merging with ABC company?

你有沒有聽說，我們的公司要和ABC公司合併？

I heard that Mary is getting married.

我聽說瑪麗就要結婚了。

A What happened to John?
  **I heard** he was fired.

B Let me put it this way, he will probably be going to jail.

A What did he do?

B He's been accused of embezzling.

A 約翰出什麼事了？
  我聽說他被開除了。

B 讓我這樣說吧，他可能就要被抓去坐牢了。

A 他做了什麼事？

B 他被控訴虧空公款。

- ☑ fire
  [faɪr]
  V. 開除

- ☑ leave
  [liv]
  離開

- ☑ company
  ['kʌmpənɪ]
  公司

- ☑ merge
  [mɝdʒ]
  合併

- ☑ probably
  ['prɑbəblɪ]
  可能地

- ☑ jail
  [dʒel]
  監獄

- ☑ embezzle
  [ɪm'bɛzḷ]
  盜用公款

- ☑ be accused of
  被控訴

- ☑ heard
  [hɝd]
  聽說（hear的過去式）

# 042

# What I really like is ~

我真正喜歡的是⋯

句型 模擬站

**What I really like is a day off.**

我真正喜歡的是，放假天不用上班。

---

句型解析站

What I really like（我真正喜歡的）整個子句當主詞，後面所喜歡的事物要用名詞，例如： that pink dress 和 his speech。若是動詞要改成動名詞 Ving，例如： making a lot of money。

---

句型 連結站

What I really like is that pink dress.
我真正喜歡的是那一件粉紅色的衣服。

What I really like is his speech.
我真正喜歡的是他的演講。

What I really like is making a lot of money.
我真正喜歡的是賺很多的錢。

**A** I heard the company is planning a big party.

**B** Yes, but **what I really like is a** day off.

**A** I don't blame you.
You have worked night and day for weeks.

**B** Well, I'll go to the party.
And then I'll take a couple of days off.

☑ a day off
　放一天假

☑ speech
　[spitʃ]
　演講

☑ blame
　[blem]
　責怪

☑ a couple of
　一些

A 我聽說，公司正在計劃一個大型的宴會。

B 不過，我真正喜歡的是放一天假，不用上班。

A 這也難怪你。
好幾星期以來，你都是日以繼夜的工作。

B 是呀，我會去參加宴會。
然後，我要休幾天的假。

## 043

# Maybe ~

也許…

MP3-44

**句型 模擬站**

**Maybe** I should give it a try.

也許我應該試一試。

**句型解析站**

　　說話時，有時我們會提個建議，此時的語氣應該與命令句，一般的肯定句或疑問句不同，先以 Maybe 也許起頭，充分表達了你只是提建議的語氣。

**句型 連結站**

Maybe we should call it a day.

也許我們今天應該到此為止。

Maybe I should ask him to explain.

也許我應該要求他解釋。

Maybe you should say "sorry" to her.

也許你應該向她說「抱歉」。

**A** We took the kids to roller blade
yesterday.
It was fun.

**B** I've thought about doing that.
But I'm afraid of falling.

**A** I didn't fall at all.
It is the same as roller skating.
You're good at that.

**B** **Maybe** I should give it a try.

A 我們昨天帶小孩去玩滑輪刀。
那很好玩。

B 我也想到那麼做。
不過，我怕摔跤。

A 我從頭到尾，都沒有摔跤。
它就跟普通滑輪溜冰一樣。
你的技術很好的。

B 也許我應該試一試。

☑ maybe
['mebi]
也許

☑ should
[ʃʊd]
應該

☑ explain
[ɪk'splen]
解釋

☑ roller blade
['rolɚ bled]
滑輪刀遊戲

☑ fall
[fɔl]
跌倒

☑ roller skating
['rolɚ 'sketɪŋ]
溜滑輪

☑ be good at ~
很行

# 044

## crazy about ~
### 對…很著迷

MP3-45

**句型 模擬站**

I'm **crazy about** it.
我對它很著迷。

**句型解析站**

> crazy about 表示（對某件東西，或事物）很著迷，很熱中，這是口語中的用法。若說（對某事）並不熱中或著迷，說法是 not crazy about。

**句型 連結站**

He is crazy about the video game.
他對電動玩具很著迷。

I'm not crazy about opera.
我對歌劇不是很熱衷。

She is crazy about rock-and-roll.
她對搖滾樂很著迷。

**A** How do you like your new car?

**B** I'm **crazy about** it.
I waited a long time for a sports car.

**A** How many seats does it have?

**B** Only two.
That's one of the best things about it!

A 你還喜歡你的新車吧？

B 我對它很著迷。
我要一部跑車，等了好久了。

A 它有幾個座位？

B 只有二個座位。
那是它最大的優點之一。

☑ crazy
['krezɪ]
著迷的；熱中的

☑ video game
['vɪdɪ͵o gem]
電動玩具

☑ opera
['ɑpərə]
歌劇

☑ rock-and-roll
['rɑkən'rol]
搖滾樂

☑ sports car
['sports kɑr]
跑車

☑ seat
[sit]
座位

# 045

## Could you ~
### 可否請你…

**句型 模擬站**

**Could you do me a big favor?**
可否請你幫我個忙？

**句型解析站**

　　當你想請別人為你做件事時，用Could you，或Would you起頭都可以。

**句型 連結站**

Could you tell me the time?
可否請你告訴我時間？

Could you close the window, please?
可否請你幫忙關上窗子？

Could you show me where the rest room is?
可否請你告訴我，洗手間在那裡？

**A** Diana, **could you** do me a big favor?

**B** If I can.

**A** I've got a doctor's appointment next Thursday.
Would you watch the kids for me?

**B** Sure, what time?

**A** My appointment is at 2:00.
Will that work?

**B** Yes, that's fine.
I'd be glad to watch them for you.

☑ favor
　['fevɚ]
　恩惠

☑ rest room
　洗手間；休息室

☑ appointment
　[ə'pɔɪntmənt]
　約好時間，預定
　時間

A 戴安娜，能不能請你幫個忙？
B 只要我可以。
A 我下星期四要看醫生。
　你能不能幫我看小孩？
B 當然，幾點？
A 我約的是兩點鐘。
　可以嗎？
B 可以，沒有問題。
　我很樂意幫你看小孩。

MP3-47

# Is everything ~?

所有一切都…嗎？

## Is everything okay?

所有一切都還好嗎？

### 句型解析站

在很多情況下，你都可能遇到要問對方是不是一切情況都很好，或是，是否一切都在掌握之下等等問候的話。記住這個句型，Is everything再接你要問的情況。

### 句型 連結站

## Is everything all right?

所有一切都還好嗎？

## Is everything under control?

所有一切，都在掌握之中嗎？

## Is everything fine?

所有一切，都好嗎？

**A** What's going on?

**B** Nothing.
Why do you ask like that?

**A** You look really stressed out.
**Is everything** okay?

**B** Yes. I'm just tired.
I've been working late every night.

---

☑ control
[kən'trol]
控制

☑ fine
[faɪn]
很好

☑ stress
[strɛs]
壓力

☑ tired
[taɪrd]
疲倦的

---

A 發生了什麼事？

B 沒什麼。
你為什麼這麼問呢？

A 你看起來，壓力很大的樣子。
所有一切，都還好吧？

B 是的，我只是比較疲倦而已。
我每天晚上都工作到很晚。

## 047

MP3-48

# I don't have the foggiest idea ~

我對…一點概念都沒有。

**句型 模擬站**

**I don't have the foggiest idea** what he was talking about.

我對他所說的，一點概念都沒有。

**句型解析站**

foggiest 是 foggy 的最高級，foggy 這個字用來說明 idea（概念；觀點時），是「模糊的、混淆的」的意思。所以，當你遇到一件事，你真的都不知道時，可以說 I don't have the foggiest idea.（我實在是一點概念也沒有。）

**句型 連結站**

I don't have the foggiest idea how to do it.

我對於到底要怎麼做一點概念都沒有。

I don't have any idea what he was talking about.

我對他所說的，沒什麼概念。

I don't have the foggiest idea when the plane will take off.

我對於飛機幾時起飛，一點概念都沒有。

☑ foggy
['fɑgɪ]
模糊的

☑ idea
[aɪ'diə]
概念

☑ take off
起飛

☑ lecture
['lɛktʃɚ]
講課

☑ understand
[ˌʌndɚ'stænd]
瞭解（過去式 understood）

☑ professor
[prə'fɛsɚ]
教授

## 會話 轉播站

**A** Did you understand Professor Young's lecture?

- - - - - - - - - - - - - - - - - - - - - - - - -

**B** No. **I don't have the foggiest idea** what he was talking about.

- - - - - - - - - - - - - - - - - - - - - - - - -

**A** Neither do I.
And I haven't found anyone else who understood it.

- - - - - - - - - - - - - - - - - - - - - - - - -

**B** Well, we'll just have to ask him to explain it again tomorrow.

- - - - - - - - - - - - - - - - - - - - - - - - -

A 你瞭解楊教授所講的課嗎？

B 不，我對他講的一點概念都沒有。

A 我也沒有。
而且，我找不到任何其他瞭解的人。

B 是嗎，那我們明天要求他再解釋一次。

## 048

MP3-49

# ~ new one ~

## 那還是新聞

句型 模擬站

**That's a new one on me.**

那對我來講，還是個新聞。

### 句型解析站

當有人說了一件事，你並不知道時，可以用 That's a new one on me. That's news to me. 或是 I didn't know that. 這三句話表示「我沒聽說過這件事」的意思。

句型 連結站

**I didn't know that.**

我還不知道有這回事。

**That's news to me.**

那對我來講是新聞。

**That's something else.**

那真是意想不到。

**A** I'll see you tomorrow.

**B** Tomorrow?
What's tomorrow?

**A** We have a special board meeting.

**B** That's a **new one** on me.
What time and where?

☑ new
[nju]
新的

☑ news
[njuz]
新聞

☑ special
['spɛʃəl]
特別的

☑ board
[bord]
董事會

☑ meeting
['mitɪŋ]
會議

A 明天見。

B 明天？
什麼明天？

A 我們明天召開一個特別董事會。

B 那對我來講，還是個新聞。
什麼時間，什麼地點呢？

**MP3-50**

# 049

# trick
秘訣

I know there's a **trick** to it.
我知道一定有秘訣的。

### 句型解析站

　　trick 這個字指「訣竅；招數；秘訣」的意思。the trick of ~ 指「做某事的秘訣」，of 的後面接動名詞 Ving。There's a trick to it. 指「做某事有個竅門」。

句型 連結站

I know the trick of riding backwards.
我知道倒騎腳踏車的秘訣。

Do you know any trick of cutting the cost?
你知道什麼降低成本的秘訣嗎？

I used up all the tricks I know.
我已經把我懂的招數都用盡了。

**A** I can't get this bracelet fastened. Can you help me?

**B** Sure. What's the problem?

**A** I'm not sure.
I know there's a **trick** to it, but I can't figure it out.

**B** Ah, here it is.
You have to push and twist at the same time.

A 我不能把這個手環扣緊。
你能幫我忙嗎？

B 當然，出了什麼問題？

A 我不清楚。
我知道一定有秘訣，但是我想不起來。

B 啊，在這裡。
你必須要同時向下按而且轉一下。

☑ trick
[trɪk]
秘訣；訣竅

☑ backwards
[ˈbækwɚdz]
往後的

☑ use up
用盡

☑ bracelet
[ˈbreslɪt]
手鐲

☑ fasten
[ˈfæsn̩]
扣緊

☑ problem
[ˈprɑbləm]
問題

☑ figure
[ˈfɪgjɚ]
想出

☑ twist
[twɪst]
轉

☑ at the same time
同時

MP3-51

# *050* Anything I can ~?

## 有沒有什麼我可以…的？

句型 模擬站

## Anything I can help you with?

有沒有什麼我可以幫你忙的？

句型解析站

Anything I can help you with? 這句話完整的句型是 Is there anything I can help you with? 句中的 Is there 省略掉，常用在口語中。

句型 連結站

Anything I can do for you?

有沒有什麼我可以幫你做的？

Anything I can show you?

有沒有什麼，我可以展示給你的？

Let me know if there is anything I can help you with.

如果有什麼我可以幫你的，請讓我知道。

**A** The party's great.
What are you doing back here in the kitchen?

------------------------------------------

**B** I have a few things to finish.

------------------------------------------

**A** **Anything I can** help you with?

------------------------------------------

**B** Sure. There's a salad in the refrigerator.
Please set it on the buffet.

------------------------------------------

☑ kitchen
['kɪtʃɪn]
廚房

☑ salad
['sæləd]
沙拉

☑ refrigerator
[rɪ'frɪdʒəˌretɚ]
冰箱

☑ buffet
['bʊfeɪ]
自助餐桌

A 宴會這麼棒。
你躲在廚房做什麼？

B 我有一些事要做完。

A 有什麼我可以幫你忙的？

B 有。冰箱裡有沙拉。
請把它擺到自助餐桌上去。

## *051*

# What a ~!
多麼…的…啊！

MP3-52

### 句型 模擬站

## What a great idea!
多麼好的主意啊！

### 句型解析站

這個句型是驚嘆句，用在對某事的讚賞，句子應該是What a great idea it is! 在口語中可以把 it is 省略掉。

### 句型 連結站

What a wonderful idea!
多麼美妙的主意啊！

What a beautiful picture!
多麼漂亮的圖畫啊！

What a handsome boy!
多麼帥的男孩啊！

**A** Why don't we go to the farm and have a picnic tomorrow?

**B** **What a** great idea!

**A** I'll get the food if you will take care of the drinks.

**B** Sure. What time shall we leave?

☑ farm
[fɑrm]
農場

☑ picnic
[ˈpɪknɪk]
野餐

☑ wonderful
[ˈwʌndɚfəl]
極好的；奧妙的

☑ drink
[drɪŋk]
飲料

☑ take care of
照料

A 我們明天何不到農場去野餐？

B 多麼好的一個主意！

A 如果你願意帶飲料的話，我就準備食物。

B 當然。我們明天幾點離開呢？

## 052

MP3-53

# Believe it or not, ~

信不信由你，

## 句型 模擬站

**Believe it or not**, we won the game.

信不信由你，我們贏了這一場比賽！

## 句型解析站

Believe it or not，這句口語用在說話者要告訴對方一件事，但這件事連說話者自己都覺得不可置信，所以在告訴對方這件事之前，先加一句Believe it or not。

## 句型 連結站

Believe it or not, another typhoon is coming.

信不信由你，又有一個颱風來了。

Believe it or not, I won the lottery.

信不信由你，我中了樂透彩。

Believe it or not, we lost the game.

信不信由你，我們比賽竟然輸了。

**A** What's going on?

----------------------------------------

**B** **Believe it or not**, we won the game!

----------------------------------------

**A** Really?
The other team was so far ahead.
I thought it was hopeless.
What happened?

----------------------------------------

**B** I don't know.
Maybe we just got lucky on this one.

----------------------------------------

☑ believe
[bə'liv]
相信

☑ won
[wʌn]
贏（win的過去式）

☑ typhoon
[taɪ'fun]
颱風

☑ lottery
['lɑtərɪ]
樂透彩

☑ ahead
[ə'hɛd]
領先

A 有沒有什麼新聞？

B 信不信由你，我們比賽竟然贏了。

A 真的嗎？
對手超前這麼多。
我想已經沒希望了。
到底發生什麼事呢？

B 我不知道。
我想也許是我們的球運好吧。

# 053

## kidding

開玩笑！

MP3-54

### 句型 模擬站

**You are kidding!**
你在開玩笑！

### 句型解析站

kid 這個字當名詞，是指「小孩子」，當動詞，用在口語中的說法，有「開玩笑」或「故意愚弄」的意思，當你認為對方是故意在說笑，不是認真的，你可以說You are kidding! 表示你認為對方說的話是在開玩笑的，不是真的，或者用疑問句 Are you kidding me? 問對方是否在開玩笑。

### 句型 連結站

**Are you kidding me?**
你開我什麼玩笑？

**No kidding!**
別開玩笑了！

**You've got to be kidding.**
你一定是在開玩笑吧。

**A** We've been chosen to have a free cruise.

----

**B** You're **kidding**.

----

**A** No joke!
We really were selected.

----

**B** Wow. I hadn't expected this at all.

----

A 我們中獎了，贏了一個免費的海上旅行。

B 你在開玩笑吧。

A 才不開玩笑！
我們真的被選上了。

B 哇。我從來沒有預期會發生。

☑ kid
[kɪd]
開玩笑

☑ chosen
[ˈtʃozn̩]
選擇；挑選
（choose的過去
分詞）

☑ select
[səˈlɛkt]
挑選；選中

☑ expect
[ɪkˈspɛkt]
期待

☑ cruise
[kruz]
坐船旅行

# we met ~

## 我們在…見過面。

MP3-55

### 句型 模擬站

We met yesterday.
我們昨天見過面。

### 句型解析站

met 是 meet 的過去式和過去分詞，表「見面」的意思。We met yesterday. 中的 yesterday 是過去的時間，所以，句子用過去式。若是說「我們已經見過面了」，用現在完成式 We've met.。

### 句型 連結站

Haven't we met before?
我們以前有沒有見過面呢？

I believe we've met.
我相信我們見過面。

I don't think we've met before.
我不認為我們以前見過面。

**A** Hi, Jim. How are you?

**B** I'm okay.
How about yourself?

**A** Pretty good.
**Have you met** John?

**B** Yes, we met yesterday.
How are you, John?

☑ pretty
['prɪtɪ]
相當地

☑ yourself
你自己

A 嗨，吉姆。你好嗎？

B 還好。
你自己呢？

A 還很好。
你和約翰見過面嗎？

B 有，我們昨天就見過了。
約翰，你好嗎？

# 055

## I thought ~

我以為…

MP3-56

句型 模擬站

**I thought** they would be much shorter.

我以為他們會比較短。

句型解析站

thought 是 think 的過去式,表示「認為,以為」的意思,所以,句子若以 I thought 起頭時,是在強調你原本的想法,但卻發現事實並非如你所想的。

句型 連結站

I thought you could do a better job.
我以為你的表現會更好。

I thought Mr. Wang could help us.
我以為王先生會幫我們的忙。

I thought he would be friendlier since we met yesterday.
我以為我們昨天見過面,他會比較友善。

**A** Boy, are the lines long today!

**B** Yes, **I thought** they would be much shorter since school has started.

**A** Actually I think they are.
The line for the roller coaster was much longer when we were here in July.

A 唉呀,今天真是大排長龍。

B 是呀,我想學校既然開學了,排的隊應該短一點。

A 事實上,我想是比較短。
我們七月來的時候,雲霄飛車所排的隊比現在還長的多呢。

☑ friendlier
['frɛndlɪɚ]
較友善些
(friendly的比較級)

☑ boy
唉呀!(感嘆語)

☑ line
[laɪn]
隊伍

☑ actually
['æktʃʊəlɪ]
實際上

4 roller coaster
['rolɚ 'kostɚ]
雲霄飛車

☑ thought
[θɔt]
認為;以為
(think的過去式)

MP3-57

# 056

# It took hours to ~

那要好幾個小時才…

**句型 模擬站**

## It took hours to complete.

那要好幾個小時，才做得完。

**句型解析站**

It 是虛主詞，真正的主詞是時間後面的不定詞，例如：to complete，所以是去做某件事要花這些時間的。

**句型 連結站**

It took days to finish.
那要好幾天，才做得完。

It took weeks to be done.
那要好幾個禮拜才做得成。

How long did it take you to fix it ?
你一共花了多少時間才修好？

**A** The kid's costumes look great.

**B** Thanks. **It took hours to** complete.

**A** The trim really makes the costume.

**B** I guess.
But I don't know if all the extra effort is worth it.

---

A 這些小孩的服裝，看起來真漂亮。

B 謝謝你。我花了好幾個小時才做完的。

A 這些花邊，真的讓這件服裝很出色。

B 我想是吧。
不過，額外花了這麼多工，我不知道是否值得。

☑ took
[tʊk]
花（時間）
（take 的過去式）

☑ complete
[kəm'plit]
完成

☑ finish
['fɪnɪʃ]
完成

☑ fix
[fɪks]
修理

☑ costume
['kɑstjum]
服裝

☑ trim
[trɪm]
花邊

☑ extra
['ɛkstrə]
額外的

## 057

# Did you hear about ~?

### 你聽說…了嗎？

MP3-58

# Did you hear about the new bookstore?

你聽說過那家新書店了嗎？

### 句型解析站

　　當你問對方是否聽說某件事了，就用 Did you hear about這句型來問。介系詞 about 後面要加名詞當受詞，例如：the new bookstore, the new plan.。

### 句型 連結站

Did you hear about the new project?
你聽說過那個新企劃案嗎？

Did you hear about the new plan?
你聽說過那個新的計劃嗎？

Did you hear about the new rule?
你聽說過那個新的規則嗎？

**A** Did you hear about the new bookstore?

----

**B** The one with the coffee shop in it?

----

**A** Yes. It is the neatest place.

----

☑ bookstore
['buk,stor]
書店

☑ project
['pradʒɛkt]
企劃

☑ rule
[rul]
規則

☑ neat
[nit]
很棒的（最高級 neatest）

A 你聽說過那個新書店嗎？

B 就是那間裡面有咖啡座的？

A 是的。那個地方真的不錯。

## 058

MP3-59

# sometime in ~
在…的某個時候

### 句型 模擬站

We're talking about **sometime in** May.
我們所說的是五月的某個時候。

---

#### 句型解析站

sometime當副詞，指「未來某個時候」，若計劃中已有一個大略的時間，例如在某月、或是在夏天、在明年等等，但還沒確切的日期時，就說 sometime in 已知的大略時間。

---

### 句型 連結站

We're planning on sometime in May.
我們計畫在五月裡的某個時候。

We're talking about going on vacation sometime in the summer.
我們在談論夏天裡，找個時間去度假。

We are not talking about now, but sometime in May.
我們談的不是現在，而是5月裡的某個時候。

**A** John asked me to marry him.

**B** That's great!
Have you set a date?

**A** We're talking about **sometime in** May.

☑ set
[sɛt]
訂好

☑ date
[det]
日期

☑ talking about
討論計畫

A 約翰向我求婚。

B 那太好了！
結婚日期訂好了嗎？

A 我們計劃在5月裡的某一天。

## 059

# Where is ~?

…在那裡？

MP3-60

## Where is the new office?

新的辦公室在那裡呢？

### 句型解析站

這是問「在那裡？」的疑問句句型，用 Where is
起頭，後面接你要問的地方。

### 句型 連結站

Where is your school?
你們的學校在那裡呢？

Where is the Central Library?
中央圖書館在那裡呢？

Where is your office located?
你們的辦公室在那裏呢？

**A** What is this about the company relocating?

**B** From what I understand, we will be moving in September.

**A** **Where is** the new office?

**B** Not far.
About two miles north of here on Nan-King East Road.

☑ company
[ˈkʌmpənɪ]
公司

☑ understand
[ˌʌndɚˈstænd]
了解

☑ relocating
[rɪloˈketɪŋ]
遷到別處

☑ mile
[maɪl]
哩

A 公司搬遷這件事是怎麼一回事？

B 據我所了解的，我們九月底要搬。

A 新的辦公室在那裡呢？

B 不遠。
大概從這裡往北二哩，在南京東路上。

# *060* It will take some time to ~

那需要一段時間，才…

## 句型 模擬站

**It will take some time to get used to.**

那需要一段時間才能習慣。

### 句型解析站

take 是花（時間），cost 是花（金錢）。其句型用法是 It will take（時間）to ~。和 It will cost（金錢）to ~。

## 句型 連結站

**It will take some time to build a new one.**

蓋一個新的，那需要一段時間。

**It will take some time to finish this work.**

把這個工作做完，需要一段時間。

**It will take some time to change his mind.**

改變他的主意，需要一段時間。

It will cost me a lot to install the new equipment.
把新的設備裝起來，需要一段時間。

☑ get used to
習慣

☑ build
[bɪld]
建造

☑ different
[ˈdɪfrənt]
不同的

**會話 轉播站**

**A** How do you like your new school?

**B** I don't know.
It's different.

**A** It will take some time to get used to.

**B** I know.

A 你喜歡你的新學校嗎？

B 我不知道。
是那樣的不同。

A 那要花一段時間才能習慣。

B 我知道。

# 061

## What about ~?

### 你認為…如何？

**What about a cassette player for her car?**

你認為買一個卡式播放機，放在她的車上如何？

句型解析站

　　你提出一個提議，問對方的看法如何時，用 What about再接你所提出的建議。

句型 連結站

What about a new watch for her birthday?

你認為買一個新手錶，送她當生日禮物如何？

What about a red shirt for the party?

你認為穿紅襯衫參加宴會如何？

What about a new table for the dining room?

你認為餐廳擺個新餐桌如何？

**A** I don't know what to get Mom for her birthday.

------------------------------------------------

**B** **What about** a cassette player for her car?

------------------------------------------------

**A** That's a great idea.

------------------------------------------------

☑ cassette
[kə'sɛt]
卡式

☑ cassette player
卡式播放機

☑ dinning room
餐廳

A 我不知道媽媽生日時,該送她什麼禮物。

B 你認為買個卡式播放機,放在她車上如何?

A 那是個好主意。

# 062

# help ~ with
幫…忙

**句型 模擬站**

Is there anything I can **help** you **with**?

有沒有可以幫你忙的呀？

---

**句型解析站**

當你想提供你的幫助時，可以問 Is there anything I can help you with? 或是 Is there anything I can do for you?

---

**句型 連結站**

Is there anything I can do for you?
有沒有什麼我可以幫你忙的？

Would you help me with the report?
你願意幫我寫報告嗎？

Mary asked me to help her with filing.
瑪麗要求我幫她整理檔案。

**A** It looks like that's giving you some problems.

**B** A bunch of them.

**A** Is there anything I can **help** you **with**?

**B** Sure. Hold this piece while I hammer.

A 看來，它給你帶來一些困難。

B 困難可多呢。

A 有沒有我可以幫忙的？

B 當然。在我敲鐵鎚的時候，請把這個東西握好。

☑ report
[rɪˈport]
報告

☑ filing
[ˈfaɪlɪŋ]
整理檔案

☑ a bunch of
許多；很多

☑ hold
[hold]
拿好

☑ hammer
[ˈhæmɚ]
（用鐵鎚）鎚打

# How was ~?

…還好吧？

MP3-64

句型 模擬站

## How was your recital?
你的獨奏會進行得還好吧？

句型解析站

當你問對方某件事進行得如何時，那件事已經發生過了，所以要用過去式be動詞「was」來問。

句型 連結站

How was your weekend?
你的週末過得如何呢？

How was your English test?
你的英語考試，還好吧？

How was the trip?
這一趟旅行，還好吧？

**A** How was your recital?

**B** It was good.
I got through the piece without any mistakes.

**A** I bet you're relieved.
You were really stressed out about it.

**B** You're right.
I was and I am relieved it' over.

---

☑ recital
[rɪ'saɪtl̩]
獨奏會

☑ get through
完成；度過

☑ piece
[pis]
整首樂曲

☑ mistake
[mɪ'stek]
錯誤

☑ relieve
[rɪ'liv]
（壓力）解除

---

A 你的獨奏會進行得如何？

B 進行得很好。
我從頭彈到尾都沒有出錯。

A 我想你是鬆了一口氣了。
這個演奏，給你帶來的壓力很大。

B 你說的一點都沒錯。
我的壓力很大，而且現在過了，我覺得很輕鬆。

MP3-65

# ~ should be ~
## …應該是…

**句型 模擬站**

## That **should be** fun.
那應該是很好玩的。

**句型解析站**

當你認為某件事或某人應該是會如何時,句型是主詞 + should be,若你認為某件事或某人應該不會如何時,句型是主詞 + shouldn't be。

**句型 連結站**

## The movie should be interesting.
這部電影應該是很有趣。

## You should be happy.
你應該高興才對。

## The task shouldn't be too hard.
這個工作應該不會太難。

**A** John and I are going dancing to-morrow night.

---

**B** That **should be** fun.

---

**A** I hope so.
We haven't danced in years.

☑ interesting
['ɪntərɪstɪŋ]
有趣的

☑ should
[ʃʊd]
應該是

☑ in years
好多年了

A 約翰和我明天晚上，要去跳舞。

B 那應該是很好玩的。

A 我但願如此。
我們已經好久沒跳舞。

MP3-66

# 065

# have + p.p. for ~

已經⋯了

I **haven't seen** you **for** at least three months.

我已經至少三個月沒有見到你了。

### 句型解析站

　　説話時，若是用「for ＋ 一段時間」來表示「作」持續一段時間了，就要用現在完成式「have ＋ 過去分詞」的句型來表達。中「一段時間」之前加個at least（至少）是加強時間性的説法。

### 句型 連結站

I haven't watched TV for two weeks.
我已經二個星期沒有看電視了。

I have lived here for at least three years.
我已經住在這裡，最少有三年了。

I have known him for at least 20 years.
我已經認識他，最少有二十年了。

**A** Hi! How are you?

**B** I'm doing great.
How about you?

**A** Good. It's been ages!

**B** I know.
I **haven't seen** you **for** at least
three months.

☑ watch
[wɑtʃ]
看

☑ age
[edʒ]
年

A 嗨！你好嗎？

B 我很好。
你自己呢？

A 還好。已經好久沒見面了！

B 我知道。
我已經至少有三個月沒見到你了。

# 066

## I take it ~

### 這麼說來，我認定你是…

MP3-67

**句型 模擬站**

**I take it you are leaving.**

這麼說來，我認定你是要離開。

**句型解析站**

對方說了一句話，你從他的話中聽出他的話中另有意思。所以，你就告訴他，這麼說來，我認定你的意思是這樣。這個句型就是 I take it 再接你認為他話中的真正意思。

**句型 連結站**

I take it you don't agree.
這麼說來，我認定你是不同意。

I take it you like the job.
這麼看來，你是喜歡這個工作。

I take it you want me to do the job.
這麼說來，我看你是要我做這個工作了。

**A** I'll see you later.

**B** **I take it** you are leaving.

**A** Yes. I have a report I need to research at the library.

**B** Okay. Be careful.

☑ research
['risɜtʃ]
查資料

☑ library
['laɪˌbrɛrɪ]
圖書館

A 我們再見了。

B 這麼看來,我看你是要走了。

A 是的。我有一份報告,我必須到圖書館查資料。

B 好吧。小心點。

MP3-68

# It makes no sense to ~

做…絲毫不可理解

句型 模擬站

**It makes no sense to** wash the car now.

現在去洗車，沒有道理。

句型解析站

注意以下會話轉播站中的 Boy, is this car dirty! 這句話是驚嘆句，表示你對所看到的情況表示很驚異，但同時也在問對方是否也有同感。

句型 連結站

It makes no sense to fix dinner now.

現在做晚飯，沒有道理。

It makes no sense to have John come to the party.

邀請約翰來參加宴會，沒有道理。

It doesn't make any sense to get up so early.

那麼早起床，沒有道理。

**A** Boy, is this car dirty!

**B** Yes, it is.
I just haven't gotten around to washing it.

**A** Well, **it makes no sense to** wash the car now since the forecast calls for rain.

**B** This is true.

☑ sense
[sɛns]
道理

☑ get up
起床

☑ dirty
[ˈdɝtɪ]
骯髒的

☑ since
[sɪns]
既然

☑ forecast
[ˈforˌkæst]
氣象預測

A 啊呀，這部車真髒！

B 是的，它很髒。
我只是沒時間洗。

A 是嗎，可是現在去洗也沒有道理，因為天氣預報說今天會下雨。

B 那也是事實。

# Let's see what ~

## 讓我們試試能不能…

MP3-69

**Let's see what** we can figure out.
讓我們試試能不能想一個辦法。

句型解析站

Let's see這個用法，是美國人常用的。當你想做某件事時，加上 Let's see 表示你沒有向對方保證事情一定做得成，而只是要「試試看能不能」。若 Let's see 後面接 why ，就表示要看看到底是什麼「原因」。

句型 連結站

Let's see what I can do.
讓我們試試看，我還能為你做什麼事。

Let's see why it didn't work.
讓我們來看看，它為什麼壞了。

Let's see why it sounds so awful.
讓我們來看看，為什麼它聽起來這麼糟糕。

A We have got to cut back on some of the kids' activities.

--------------------------------------------

B Why? What's wrong?

--------------------------------------------

A It's to the point where all I do is drive kids around after school.

--------------------------------------------

B Well, **let's** talk to them.
And **see what** we can figure out.

--------------------------------------------

A 我們必須把小孩的一些活動減少。

B 為什麼？有什麼問題嗎？

A 我們已經到了一放學，我就是載著小孩團團轉。

B 是嗎，那麼我來跟他們談一談。
並且試試看能不能想出辦法來。

☑ sound
[saʊnd]
聽起來

☑ awful
[ˈɔfʊl]
可怕的

☑ activity
[ækˈtɪvətɪ]
活動，（複數形 activities）

☑ drive
[draɪv]
開車

☑ after school
放學後

☑ figure out
找出答案

147

# *069*

# There are a lot of ~
有許多…

MP3-70

**句型 模擬站**

**There are a lot of** people I haven't seen in years.

有許多人，我好久沒見面了。

---

**句型解析站**

There are 和 There is 都是「有」的意思，若後面的名詞是複數，要用 There are。若後面的名詞是單數，要用 There is。本句型的例句都是用複數名詞，例如： books, things 和 jobs，所以都必須用 There are。

---

**句型 連結站**

There are a lot of books you haven't seen yet.

有好多書，你都沒有看過。

There are a lot of things we can do.

有好多事，我們可以做的。

There are a lot of jobs you can do.

有好多工作是你能做的。

**A** Are you going to your class reunion?

**B** I think so.
**There are a lot of** people I haven't seen in years.

**A** I heard that Mary is going to be there.

**B** Really?
I haven't seen her since graduation.

☑ reunion
[rɪˈjunjən]
重聚

☑ graduation
[ˌɡrædʒʊˈeʃən]
畢業典禮

☑ job
[dʒɑb]
工作

A 你要不要參加同學會？

B 我想會去吧。
有好多人我好幾年沒見過面了。

A 我聽說瑪麗也會去。

B 真的嗎？
從畢業到現在，我一直沒見過她。

# 070

# should ~

照理應該…

## That **should** help.

照理應該有幫助的。

---

### 句型解析站

should 在本句型中的用法是指依照常理來判斷，某件事應該是會怎樣的。 should 在本句型中的用法不是指義務或命令別人該做某事的應該。

---

### 句型 連結站

## That should work.

照理說應該行得通的。

## It should do this way.

照理這樣做，應該行得通的。

## That should be fine.

照理那應該沒有問題。

**A** Everyone is all stressed out about the computer system installation.

**B** No one has any answers about what the impact is going to be.

**A** I don't have any answers.
But it is something we need to talk about.
I'll schedule a meeting for tomorrow afternoon.

**B** That **should** help.
Just make sure you really listen to their concerns.

---

A 每一個員工,對於裝電腦系統,感到壓力很大。

B 沒有人曉得裝了以後,影響會是什麼。

A 我也不知道。
不過,那是我們大家應該討論的。
我會訂明天下午召開一個會議。

B 照理那應該有幫助。
你一定要真正的去聽他們所關切的。

☑ system
['sɪstəm]
系統

☑ installation
[ˌɪnstə'leʃən]
裝置

☑ answer
['ænsɚ]
答案

☑ impact
['ɪmpækt]
影響

☑ schedule
['skɛdʒʊl]
排定時間

☑ concern
[kən'sɝn]
關切

☑ listen to
注意聽

151

# 071

## planning on ~
計劃做…

MP3-72

**Planning on** taking a nap today?
你今天打算睡個午覺嗎?

### 句型解析站

　　Planning on taking a nap today? 是指正在計劃或策劃一件事,注意介系詞是用 on,很多人誤用 in。這種句型都是口語會話中才用的句型。全句應該是 Are you planning on taking a nap today? 句中的 Are you 省略掉。

### 句型 連結站

Planning on calling in sick today?
你今天打算打電話請病假嗎?

Planning on having a vacation?
你計劃去渡假嗎?

Planning on buying a new house?
你計劃要買個新房子嗎?

**A** I'm on call tonight and all day tomorrow.

**B** You look tired already.
**Planning on** taking a nap today?

**A** I hope so.
I have patients scheduled until three, so it just depends.

**B** Take care of yourself.

A 我今天晚上和明天一整天,都要待命。

B 你現在看起來已經很累。
今天打算先睡個午覺嗎?

A 我希望可以。
我的病人今天排到三點,所以還要看情形而定。

B 你自己要多照顧你自己了。

☑ take a nap
睡個午覺

☑ on call
待命

☑ patient
[ˈpeʃənt]
病人

☑ schedule
[ˈskɛdʒʊl]
排定時間

☑ depend
[dɪˈpɛnd]
依~而決定

☑ take care of
照顧

# *072*

## What did you have in mind?
### 心裡喜歡什麼樣的…？

MP3-73

句型 模擬站

## What color did you have in mind?
你心裡面所喜歡的是什麼樣的顏色？

---

句型解析站

in mind是「心中所想的」，本句型是做服務業的人不可或缺的一句話，當客人上門時，先問一句他心裡喜歡的顏色、樣式等。客人一來認為你服務周到，二來你摸清了他的底，推銷起東西，必定得心應手。

---

句型 連結站

---

What model did you have in mind?
你心裡所喜歡的是什麼樣的機型？

What price range did you have in mind?
你心裡所預想的，是怎麼樣的價格範圍？

Did you have anything particular in mind?
你心裡面有沒有特別喜歡的東西？

**A** I need some new sandals.

**B** Wonderful.
We have quite a selection.
**What** color **did you have in mind**?

**A** I haven't thought about it.
Comfort is the main factor for me.

**B** Well, these are very comfortable.
And they come in a number of colors.

---

A 我要買一些新便鞋。

B 太好了。
我們這裡可供選擇的很多。
你心裡面,有沒有特別喜歡的顏色呢?

A 我還沒有想到那個。
舒適是我考慮的主要因素。

B 是嗎,這些都很舒適。
並且,他們的顏色也很多。

☑ model
['mɑdl̩]
機型

☑ sandal
['sændl̩]
便鞋

☑ particular
[pɚ'tɪkjəlɚ]
特定的

☑ comfort
['kʌmfɚt]
舒適

☑ range
[rendʒ]
範圍

☑ factor
['fæktɚ]
考慮因素

# 073

# You've come to ~

你算闖到…

**句型 模擬站**

## You've come to the right place.

你算闖到正確的地方了。

---

**句型解析站**

　　本句型用現在完成式，you have come to 的型式，表示你就站在我的面前，我來告訴你，看你是否運氣好，遇上貴人或是要白跑一趟。闖對了地方，就是 right place，闖錯了地方，就是對不起： wrong place，遇上可以幫你忙的，就是 right person。

---

**句型 連結站**

You've come to the right person.
你算是遇到正確的人選。

You've come to the wrong place.
你算是闖到錯誤的地點。

You are talking to the wrong person.
你告訴錯人了！我幫不上忙。

A Are you interested in anything in particular today?

B We're looking for a new sofa.

A **You've come to** the right place. We have forty different styles to choose from.

A 你今天有沒有特別喜歡的東西？

B 我們在找一套新沙發。

A 那你今天算是來到正確的地方。
我們這裡有四十種不同的樣式，可供選擇。

☑ interested
['ɪntərɪstɪd]
感到有興趣

☑ sofa
['sofə]
沙發椅

☑ forty
['fɔrtɪ]
四十（注意不是 fourty）

☑ style
[staɪl]
樣式

☑ choose from
從中選擇

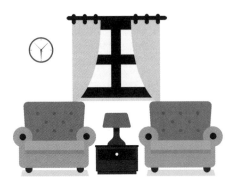

MP3-75

# I'm sure ~

我很肯定…

**句型 模擬站**

**I'm sure** we can get you a great deal.
我很肯定我們可以幫你弄到一個好的交易。

**句型解析站**

　　當你要表示你對你所要做的事很有把握時,用 I'm sure 這個句子起頭,再接你要做的事。

**句型 連結站**

I'm sure we can make you happy.
我很肯定我們會讓你高興。

I'm sure you can find the book you wanted.
我很肯定,你可以找到你想找的書。

I'm sure we can make it up to you.
我很肯定我們可以補償你。

**A** How do you like this car?

**B** I like it.
But I think it's probably too expensive.

**A** Don't worry about that.
**I'm sure** we can get you a great deal.

---

A 你喜歡這部車嗎？

B 我喜歡。
不過，我想它可能太貴了。

A 這你不用擔心。
我很確定我們可以幫你弄個好交易。

☑ deal
[dil]
交易

☑ probably
['prɑbəblɪ]
可能的

☑ expensive
[ɪk'spɛnsɪv]
昂貴的

☑ worry
['wɝɪ]
擔心

☑ make up
補償

159

MP3-76

# I really need to ~

我真的需要…

**I really need to** think about it for a few days.

我真的需要幾天時間來考慮。

說話時若要強調「一定要」時，在need的前面加個really。記住這個用法 I really need to 再接你要去做的事。

I really need to go now.
我現在真的需要走了。

I really need to talk to my boss.
我真的需要報告我的上司。

I really need to prepare for the meeting tomorrow.
我真的需要為明天的會議，準備一下。

**A** So, shall we wrap this one up for you?

----

**B** I don't think so.
**I really need to** think about it for a few days.

----

**A** You're aware that this sale ends today?
I can't hold it for you at this price after tonight.

----

**B** I may just have to wait until it's on sale again.

---

☑ a few
　一些

☑ boss
　[bɔs]
　上司；老闆

☑ prepare
　[prɪˈpɛr]
　準備

☑ wrap
　[ræp]
　包

☑ aware
　[əˈwɛr]
　注意到；知道

☑ hold
　[hold]
　保留

---

A 那麼，我們現在可以幫你把這個包裝起來了嗎？

B 暫時不用。
　我真的需要幾天的時間去考慮一下。

A 你知道拍賣今天截止嗎？
　過了今晚，我就不能用這個價錢為你保留了。

B 那我可能必須等下一次再拍賣的時候了。

## 076

MP3-77

# sounds ~ enough.

聽起來夠…了

**句型 模擬站**

## That **sounds** fair **enough**.

那聽起來夠公平了。

**句型解析站**

　　sound 這個字當「聽起來」的意思時，後面要接形容詞。enough這個字在說明一個形容詞時，要放在形容詞的後面，所以構成了 That sounds good enough 這樣的句型。

**句型 連結站**

## That sounds like a good idea.

那聽起來好像是個好主意。

## The price sounds fair enough.

這個價錢聽起來，好像是夠公道。

## The plan sounds good enough.

這個計劃，好像聽起來夠好。

**A** Why don't we split the expense for the trip?

**B** That **sounds** fair **enough**.
Shall we do the same with the new computer?

**A** Sure. Why not?

☑ fair
[fɛr]
公平的

☑ enough
[əˈnʌf]
足夠的

☑ split
[splɪt]
均分

☑ expense
[ɪkˈspɛns]
費用

☑ computer
[kəmˈpjutə]
電腦

A 這趟旅行，我們何不各分攤一半開銷？

B 那聽起來，夠公道的。
那部新的電腦，也要這麼做嗎？

A 當然，有什麼不好？

MP3-78

# 077

# beat ～

超越…

**句型 模擬站**

## We can **beat** that price.

我們可以賣得比那個價錢低。

**句型解析站**

　　beat這個字原本是超越；打敗的意思。用在beat that price，不能照字面直接翻譯成「打敗那個價錢」，而是指「出比那個更好的價錢」。若你是賣方那就表示「可以以更低的價錢來賣」，若你是買方那就表示「可以出更高的價錢來買」。

**句型 連結站**

## I can beat the deal he gave you.

我們可以用比他給你更好的條件，賣給你。

## I can't beat that.

我無法超越那個條件。

## Work harder and we can beat him.

再努力一點，我們就可以打敗他。

**A** Shall I write this up for you now?

**B** No. We found the same thing for a hundred dollars less at another store.

**A** Really? I'll tell you what.
We can **beat** that price.
Just let me verify it with the manager.

☑ beat
　[bit]
　超越

☑ verify
　['vɛrə,faɪ]
　查證

☑ manager
　['mænɪdʒɚ]
　經理

☑ harder
　[hɑrdɚ]
　更努力（hard的
　比較級）

A 我現在就可以開賬單給你了嗎？

B 不。我們在另外一家店，看到同一個東西比你便宜一塊錢。

A 真的嗎？我告訴你吧。
我們可以賣的比這個價錢低。
不過，先讓我和我的經理查證一下。

MP3-79

# *078*

# It's time to ~

是…的時候了。

句型 模擬站

**It's time for us to go home.**

是我們回家的時候了。

句型解析站

> 　　該是「做什麼事情」的時候了，用 It's time to 後面接「該做的事情」，如果說「該是我們做某事的時候了」，在 It's time to 後面先接 for us，再接「該做的事」。

句型 連結站

**It's time for us to say "No".**

是我們說「不」的時候了。

**It's time for us to get ready and go.**

是我們收拾離開的時候了。

**It's time for us to give him a lesson.**

是我們給他一個教訓的時候了。

**A** It's time for us to go home.

**B** So soon?

**A** I'm afraid so.
I have an early flight to catch.
And I still have to pack.

**B** I'm sorry you have to leave.
Have a good trip.

☑ get ready
準備好

☑ give him a lesson
給他一個教訓

☑ catch
[kætʃ]
搭火車，飛機

☑ pack
[pæk]
整理行李

☑ trip
[trɪp]
旅行

A 是我們回家的時候了。

B 這麼早啊？

A 恐怕是的。
我明天早上，很早要搭飛機。
我還要打包呢。

B 真遺憾，你要離開。
祝你一路順風。

MP3-80

# Would you care to ~?

你要不要…？

## 079

句型 模擬站

## Would you care to see it?

你要不要看呢？

### 句型解析站

要詢問對方用 Would you 做句首比用 Will you 還客氣，這是學英語的人，不可不知的，而 care 原意是「關心」，在這裡是「有心來」做某件事，所以全句就是問對方「是否有心」，也就是「要不要」的意思。看看，這個句型是不是比 Do you want to...? 更漂亮嗎？英語能力高低，差別就在這裡。

### 句型 連結站

Would you care to join us?
你要不要加入我們呢？

Would you care to give him a hand?
你要不要幫他一個忙呢？

Would you care to have a drink?
你要不要喝一杯呢？

**A** We have a two-bedroom apartment available for seven hundred a month.

**B** That sounds quite reasonable.

**A** Would you care to see it?

**B** Yes. Please show it to me.

**A** This way, please.

---

☑ give a hand
　幫忙

☑ have a drink
　喝一杯

☑ apartment
　[ə'pɑrtmənt]
　公寓

☑ reasonable
　['riznəbl̩]
　合理的

---

A 我們有二房的空公寓，七百塊一個月。

B 價格聽起來蠻合理的。

A 你要不要看一下呢？

B 好。請帶我去看。

A 請走這裡。

## 080

MP3-81

# My understanding is ~

根據我所瞭解…

句型 模擬站

**My understanding is** that we will meet at the campsite at dusk.

根據我所瞭解，黃昏的時候，我們要在露營的地點碰面。

句型解析站

當有人問你消息或資訊時，在你的回答之前加句 My understanding is，表示這是你所瞭解的情況，不一定是百分之百正確的情況。

句型 連結站

My understanding is Mary is not coming.

根據我所瞭解，瑪麗不來。

My understanding is that this has to be done by tomorrow.

根據我的瞭解，到明天之前工作要做完。

My understanding is that they are cutting budget.

根據我所瞭解，他們現在在減縮預算。

☑ campsite
['kæmp,saɪt]
營地

☑ dusk
[dʌsk]
黃昏時

☑ partner
['pɑrtnɚ]
伙伴；合夥人

☑ budget
['bʌdʒɪt]
預算

☑ as long as
只要

**會話 轉播站**

**A** We can do whatever we want to this afternoon.

**B** Right. As long as you stay with your partner.

**A** How long do we have?

**B** **My understanding is** that we will meet at the campsite at dusk.

A 我們今天下午可以自由活動。

B 是的。只要你和你的伙伴待在一起。

A 我們有多少時間呢？

B 我的瞭解是，黃昏的時候我們要在露營的地點碰面。

171

## 081

# I wonder if ~

我在想是否…

MP3-82

**句型 模擬站**

**I wonder if** there is something wrong with the drain.

我在想下水道是否有問題。

**句型解析站**

當你對某個情況不很肯定知道時，可以用 I wonder if 開始。或是當你想向朋友借東西或問消息、資訊時，也可以用 I wonder if 來做為句子的起頭，這樣的句型，雖然不是疑問句，但對方自能明白你是在問一件事情。

**句型 連結站**

I wonder if we could call him now.

我在想我們現在是否能打電話給他。

I wonder if they can make it.

我在想他們是不是能辦得到。

I wonder if I could borrow your car for the weekend.
我在想這個週末能不能借你的車。

☑ drain
[dren]
下水道

☑ floor
[flor]
地板

☑ dishwasher
[ˈdɪʃ,waʃɚ]
洗碗機

☑ overflow
[ˈovɚ,flo]
溢出

**會話 轉播站**

**A** There is water all over the floor here.

--------------------------------------------

**B** What seems to be the problem?

--------------------------------------------

**A** I'm not sure.
It looks like the dishwasher over-flowed.

--------------------------------------------

**B** **I wonder if** there is something wrong with the drain.

--------------------------------------------

A 這裡的地板都是水。

B 看起來是什麼問題呢？

A 我不確定。
看起來好像是洗碗機漏水了。

B 我在想是不是下水道有問題。

# *082*

# That's the best ~
那是最好的…；能力所及的

**句型 模擬站**

**That's the best** we can do.
那是我們能力所及，所能做的了。

**句型解析站**

　　本句型是形容詞最高級的用法。注意在形容詞的最高級，例如： best, longest 之前要加個 the。

**句型 連結站**

That's the best I can help you.
那是我能力所及，所能幫你忙的最高極限了。

That's the best movie I've ever seen.
那是我看過，最好的一部電影。

That's the longest river in the world.
那是全世界最長的河流。

**A** We will have it ready for you Friday afternoon.

**B** Friday?
I really need it as soon as possible.

**A** **That's the best** that we can do.

**B** Well, I guess I'll have to wait.

---

A 我們星期五下午，可以幫你做好。

B 星期五？
我真的需要越快越好。

A 那是我們盡能力所及，所能夠做到的極限了。

B 是嗎，我想我只好等了。

☑ best
[bɛst]
最好的（good的最高級）

☑ movie
['muvɪ]
電影

☑ river
['rɪvɚ]
河

☑ world
[wɝld]
世界

☑ ready
['rɛdɪ]
準備好

☑ possible
['pɑsəbl̩]
可能的

☑ wait
[wet]
等待

# 083

## It's not as ~ as ~

那不像…一樣的…

MP3-84

**句型 模擬站**

**It's not as** bad **as** it was yesterday.

那不像昨天的一樣糟。

**句型解析站**

　　注意這個句型裏的as ~ as是在比較過去的事情和現在的事情之間的異同，例句中是It's（今天的天氣）不像 it was yesterday（昨天）的一樣的糟。

**句型 連結站**

It's not as hot as it was yesterday.

天氣不像昨天一樣熱。

It's not as good as I expected.

它不像我昨天預期的一樣好。

It's not as wet as it was last year.

氣候不像去年一樣潮濕。

**A** What is wrong with the computer system?
I have a huge backlog of reports.

------

**B** It's really overloaded right now.
But, **it's not as** bad **as** it was yesterday.

------

**A** I was out of the office yesterday.
What happened?

------

**B** The whole system locked up.
We're going to have to upgrade pretty quick.

------

A 電腦系統怎麼了？
我的電腦報表，積壓很多。

B 電腦現在負荷過重。
不過，現在情形沒有昨天的糟糕。

A 昨天我不在辦公室。
發生什麼事了？

B 所有的系統都當機。
我們真的需要趕快把電腦升級才行。

☑ expect
[ɪk'spɛkt]
期待

☑ wet
[wɛt]
潮溼

☑ huge
[hjudʒ]
巨大的

☑ backlog
['bæklɔg]
積壓

☑ report
[rɪ'port]
報告

☑ overload
['ovɚ'lod]
負荷過多

☑ lock up
卡死

☑ upgrade
['ʌp'gred]
產品升級

☑ pretty
['prɪtɪ]
相當地

☑ quick
[kwɪk]
快

# 084

MP3-85

# Excuse me, ~

對不起，…

**Excuse me, this isn't what I asked for.**

對不起，這不是我所要的。

### 句型解析站

Excuse me，這個詞不是真正在向對方道歉的用法，而是用在想提一件事之前，先說句Excuse me來向對方打聲招呼，如此，對方才會注意到你要對他說話。

### 句型 連結站

Excuse me, this isn't what you told me.
對不起，這跟你告訴我的不一樣。

Excuse me, this isn't what I ordered.
對不起，這不是我訂的貨。

Excuse me, this isn't what I expected.
對不起，這不是我預期的。

**A** **Excuse me**, this isn't what I asked for.

**B** I'm sorry.
Didn't you say you wanted the general ledger for last month?

**A** No. I need the year end general ledger.
I'm working on audit papers.

**B** Sorry. I'll get it for you right away.

☑ order
['ɔrdɚ]
點菜；訂貨

☑ ledger
['lɛdʒɚ]
總帳

☑ audit
['ɔdɪt]
審核；查帳

☑ right away
立刻

A 對不起，這不是我要的。

B 對不起。
你不是說你要上個月的流水總帳嗎？

A 不。我需要的是年底的總帳。
我正在做審核報表呢。

B 對不起。我馬上拿來。

# 085

## have ~ + p.p.
把…做了…

MP3-86

**Have you had the battery checked?**
你有沒有把電瓶檢查了？

句型解析站

　　這個句型要注意兩點，第一是，問對方「某件事做了嗎？」，用現在完成式have you had，第二是，had是使役動詞後面接「東西，事物」之後，要接過去分詞，如例句中，had the battery checked 讓電瓶被檢查句中的 checked 是過去分詞。

句型 連結站

**Have you had the car washed?**
你有沒有把車洗了？

**Have you had the dog checked up?**
你有沒有把狗帶去做健康檢查了？

**Have you had your TV set fixed?**
你有沒有把電視機修好了？

**A** What's wrong?

**B** I'm having a problem with my car.
It doesn't want to start in the morning.

**A** **Have** you **had** the battery checked?

**B** Not yet.
I'm going to take it to the shop later today.

☑ check up
健康檢查

☑ battery
[ˈbætərɪ]
電池

☑ check
[tʃɛk]
檢查

☑ start
[stɑrt]
汽車發動

A 怎麼了？

B 我的車子有問題。
今天早上，它都發動不了。

A 你有沒有把電瓶，做個檢查？

B 還沒有。
今天稍後，我會把它送到修車場去。

# 086

## ~ don't know about that.

### 認為不妥當

MP3-87

**句型 模擬站**

## I don't know about that.

我認為不妥當。

**句型解析站**

　　學英語絕對不是靠一本字典可以學好的，一定要有一本解說詳盡，並且沒有洋涇濱式句子的課本。像本句，是英美人士每日必用的語言，特別是政商界，交換意見多的場合，表示同意或反對多的場合；它的原意是「不知道」，但其實是婉轉地表示「不同意」，推說是不知道而已。下面的三個說法，全部是同一種用法，以沈吟推託表示不同意啦！

**句型 連結站**

## I am not sure about that.

我認為不妥當。

## I don't feel comfortable about that.

我認為不妥當。

## I feel funny about that.

我認為不妥當。

**A** Mom, may I go to Mary's after school today?

**B** **I don't know about that.**
You have been having trouble getting all your homework done.

**A** But it's Friday.
And we don't have any assignments for the weekend.

**B** Well, all right.
But be home by five thirty for dinner.

☑ feel comfortable
感到舒適

☑ funny
[ˈfʌnɪ]
奇怪；滑稽

☑ Mary's
瑪莉的家（所有格表示住處）

☑ assignment
[əˈsaɪnmənt]
家庭作業

A 媽媽，我今天放學後能不能去瑪麗的家？

B 我看不妥當。
你一直都沒辦法把你的家庭作業做完。

A 可是今天是星期五。
而且我們整個週末，都沒有家庭作業。

B 那，好吧。
不過，五點半要回來吃晚飯。

MP3-88

# 087

# I can't believe ~

我對⋯真難以置信。

## 句型 模擬站

**I can't believe** that they are having twins.

我對他們生雙胞胎,真是難以置信。

### 句型解析站

believe 是「相信」的意思,I can't believe 是「我不能、不敢相信」,本句型從 believe 之後出現的 that 起才是主題所在,指讓我難以置信的事,說話時,把 that省略不說也沒關係。

## 句型 連結站

I can't believe that a company like his could make money.
像他那樣的公司都可以賺錢,我實在感到不可思議。

I can't believe that they are getting married.
我對他們即將結婚,感到不可置信。

I can't believe that they didn't get hurt in the accident.
他們在這個意外當中沒有受傷,真是令人難以置信。

**A** I can't believe that they are having twins.

**B** I'm not that surprised.
John is a twin and Mary has twin sisters.

**A** I guess twins do run in families. But, when you already have three children, two more is a lot more.

**B** Yes, but fortunately they have a big house.

☑ make
money
賺錢

☑ hurt
[hɝt]
受傷

☑ twins
雙胞胎

☑ families
家庭（family的複數形）

☑ fortunately
['fɔrtʃənɪtlɪ]
幸運地

A 他們竟然生了雙胞胎，我真不敢相信。

B 我倒不是那麼驚訝。
約翰本身就是雙胞胎，而且瑪麗也有雙胞胎的姊姊。

A 我猜雙胞胎真是家傳產物。
不過，當你已經有三個小孩，再加二個實在是太多了。

B 是的，不過幸運的是，他們有很大的房子。

# 088

# How ~ were you?
你有多麼…呢？

句型 模擬站

## How late were you?
你有多麼晚呢？

句型解析站

問有多麼怎樣時，用這個句型。例如：多早（How early）、多糟（How bad）、多失望（How disappointed）。

句型 連結站

How early were you?
你是多麼早呢？

How bad was it?
情形有多糟糕呢？

How disappointed were you?
你有多失望呢？

**A** Did you pick up Mary from practice?

**B** Well, not exactly.
I was running late.
And she had already left with Jenny.

**A** **How** late **were you**?

**B** Thirty minutes.
But Jenny's mother said she would bring her home later.
They are working on their homework.

☑ disappointed
[ˌdɪsəˈpɔɪntɪd]
感到失望

☑ pick up
用汽車接人

☑ work on
從事

A 瑪麗練習之後，你有沒有接她回來？

B 噢，沒有。
我晚了一點。
她已經跟珍妮一起走了。

A 你晚了多久呢？

B 三十分鐘。
不過，珍妮的媽媽說，她稍後會帶她回家。
他們二人現在在做家庭作業。

# *089* your position on ~

你對於…的立場

MP3-90

**句型 模擬站**

I understand **your position**.

我瞭解你的立場。

**句型解析站**

position 這個字用在某些場合很好用，記住這個字，當你想在一個問題上問對方的立場時，別苦思半天想不出如何問。

**句型 連結站**

I need to know your position on the issue.

我須要知道你在這個問題的立場。

What is your position on aid to another country?

你對援助其他國家的立場是什麼？

Your position on the issue is different from mine.

你在這個問題上的立場，跟我的不同。

**A** I can not tolerate this kind of gossip.

It is very destructive.

---

**B** I understand **your position**.

How are we going to stop it?

---

**A** Very simple.

We are going to call a staff meeting.

---

**B** I hope it works.

---

☑ position

[pə'zɪʃən]

立場

☑ issue

['ɪʃʊ]

問題

☑ gossip

['gɑsəp]

私下傳聞；是非傳聞

☑ destructive

[dɪ'strʌktɪv]

毀滅性的；破壞性的

☑ staff

[stæf]

職員

A 我不能忍受這種私下傳聞。

那是非常富有破壞性的。

B 我瞭解你的立場。

我們應該怎麼樣，才能阻止這樣的傳聞呢？

A 很簡單。

我們要召開一個同仁會議。

B 我希望這會有功效。

MP3-91

## 090 put in an appearance ~

在…短暫露面。

We may **put in an appearance**.

我們也許會短暫露面一下。

### 句型解析站

appearance 是出現、露面的意思。 put in an ap-pearance這個片語是指到某地停留很短暫的時間，也就是「露面一下」的意思。

### 句型 連結站

He just put in an appearance in the meeting and soon left.

他只是在會議當中短暫露面一下，很快就會離開了。

I couldn't stay for the whole party, so I just put in an appearance and left.

我沒有辦法全程參加宴會，所以我只是短暫露面一下就離開了。

Even if you can't stay for the whole thing, at least put in an appearance.
即使你不能全程參加，你最少也要露個面。

☑ appearance
[ə'pɪrəns]
出現；露面

☑ whole
[hol]
全部的

☑ at least
至少

☑ stop by
到某地做短暫的
拜訪

☑ a little while
一下子

**會話 轉播站**

**A** Are you going to the office party tonight?

--------

**B** I don't think so.
Today is my husband's birthday.

--------

**A** I hope you stop by for a little while at least.

--------

**B** We may **put in an appearance.**

--------

A 你今天晚上，要不要參加我們公司的宴會呢？

B 我想不了。
今天是我先生的生日。

A 我希望最少你能來參加一下。

B 也許我們會短暫露面一下吧。

# 091

## be available
有…可賣嗎？

### 句型 模擬站

**Do you have any available?**
你有沒有這個東西賣呢？

### 句型解析站

　　這是一個最常用的字，但也因為太常用，可以解釋的意義太多，導致available這個英文單字讓外國人記不起來。它的涵意是「可得的」，當問一件東西是否available，可能是問有沒有「現貨」賣，或是還有沒有那件東西，而用在人的時候，可能是問該人是否有空。國人學英語，應該要在各種場合多用這個句型，將它確實駕馭善用。

### 句型 連結站

**Is the manager available?**
經理有沒有空呢？

**Do you have any smaller one available?**
你有沒有比較小的，可以賣呢？

This style is available in three sizes.
這裡賣的這個樣式，有三種尺寸。

單字 片語加油站

☑ available
[ə'veləbl̩]
可得的

☑ crystal
['krɪstl̩]
水晶的

☑ decanter
[dɪ'kæntɚ]
玻璃洋酒瓶

**會話 轉播站**

**A** Hello, may I help you find something?

**B** I'm looking for a crystal decanter. Do you **have** any **available**?

**A** Yes. We have a good selection. They are right over here.

A 你好，我可以幫你找什麼東西嗎？

B 我正在找一個水晶洋酒瓶。
你這裡有這個東西賣嗎？

A 有的。我們這裡可供選擇的很多。
他們都擺在這裡。

# I saw ~ saying ~

我看到…寫著…

MP3-93

**句型 模擬站**

## I saw your sign saying "free kittens".

我看到你外面一個招牌寫著：「免費贈送小貓。」

**句型解析站**

> I saw（我看到）可接現在分詞，例如saying，或由 that 所帶出來的子句，例如，that you are hiring。

**句型 連結站**

I saw your sign saying "Help wanted".

我看到你外面一個牌子寫著：「徵人。」

I saw in the paper that you are hiring.

我在報紙上看到你們在徵人。

I saw your sign saying the house is for sale.

我看到你們的牌子寫著有房子要賣。

**A** I **saw** your sign **saying** "free kittens".
Do you have any left?

**B** Yes, we still have three.
Would you like to see them?

**A** Let me go get my daughter.
She is the cat lover.
I'll be back in about five minutes.

**B** That's fine.
We'll be here.

---

A 我看到你的牌子寫著「免費贈送小貓」。
你還有剩下的嗎？

B 有的，我們還有三隻。
你要不要看看呢？

A 讓我去把我的女兒帶來。
她很喜歡貓的。
我五分鐘以內就回來。

B 好吧。
我們會一直在這裡的。

☑ sign
[saɪn]
牌子

☑ paper
[ˈpepɚ]
報紙

☑ free
[fri]
免費的

☑ kitten
[ˈkɪtn̩]
小貓

☑ left
[lɛft]
剩下

☑ daughter
[ˈdɔtɚ]
女兒

☑ hiring
[ˈhaɪrɪŋ]
僱用人（hire的現在分詞）

☑ for sale
要出售

# 093

# Which ~?

那一項…呢？

MP3-94

**Which** one should I apply for?

我應該申請那一項呢？

> which 是「那一個」的意思，可以加個名詞，如 which book （那一本書）， which way （那一條路）或 which model（那一型）。

Which book should I read first?

我首先應該先讀那一本書呢？

Which way should I go?

我應該走那一條路呢？

Which model should I pick?

我應該選那一個機型呢？

**A** Hello, I understand you have several nursing positions available.

**B** Yes, we do.
I have several levels of entry.

**A** **Which** one should I apply for?

**B** That would depend upon your experience.

- ☑ pick
  [pɪk]
  挑選

- ☑ several
  [ˈsɛvərəl]
  一些

- ☑ nursing
  [ˈnɝsɪŋ]
  醫護的

- ☑ position
  [pəˈzɪʃən]
  職位

- ☑ entry
  [ˈɛntrɪ]
  入門

- ☑ apply for
  申請

- ☑ model
  [ˈmɑdl]
  機型

A 你好，我知道你們這裡有幾個護士的空缺。

B 是的，我們是在找人。
我這裡有不同職等的護士。

A 我應該申請那一個呢？

B 那要看你的經驗而定。

# I have ~ for ~

我有…要…

MP3-95

**I have** some questions **for** him.

我有一些問題，要問他。

　　若說「我有個什麼東西要給某某人」，記住這個句型I have某件東西for某人。

I have mail for him.

我有郵件要給他。

I have a present for you.

我有一個禮物要給你。

I have job for you to do.

我有一個工作要你去做。

**A** May I help you?

---

**B** Could you tell me where Dr. Chen is?

---

**A** He is in room 304 with a patient right now.
May I help you?

---

**B** No, thank you.
**I have** some medical questions **for** him.

---

☑ mail
[mel]
郵件

☑ job
[dʒɑb]
工作

☑ medical
['mɛdɪkḷ]
醫學的；醫藥的

☑ question
['kwɛstʃən]
問題

---

A 有什麼需要幫忙的？

B 可以告訴我，陳醫生在什麼地方嗎？

A 他現在在304號房看病人。
我可以幫你忙嗎？

B 不，謝謝你。
我有些醫藥上的問題要問他。

# 095

## Here ~

### …在這裡

MP3-96

**句型** **模擬站**

**Here they are.**

他們都在這裡。

**句型解析站**

　　Here 起頭的句型有兩種意思，可以表示「在這裡」，也可以用在遞東西給別人時，約略有「這就是，拿走吧」的含意。在下面，這兩種意思的例句都列出來了，請仔細思考它們的使用場合吧！

**句型** **連結站**

**Here you are.**

原來你在這裡。

**Here is the book you are looking for.**

這就是你要找的那本書。

**Here is my card.**

請接受我的名片。

**A** Do you have any books about flying?

**B** Yes, **here** they are.
Is there anything in particular you are looking for?

**A** No, I'll just browse and see what's here.

**B** Let me know if I can be of any help.

☑ fly
[flaɪ]
飛行

☑ browse
[braʊz]
瀏覽

☑ of help
有幫助的

☑ card
[kɑrd]
名片

A 你這裡有沒有有關飛行的書呢？

B 有的，它們都在這裡。
你有沒有特別在找那一本呢？

A 沒有，我只是一本一本的看你們這裡有些什麼。

B 如果有需要我幫忙的話，請讓我知道。

**MP3-97**

# 096

# same
## 相同

## Same here.
我也是。

### 句型解析站

在前面學過 the same ~ as 的句型,表示「與……相同」,文法上叫做同級比較。這裡學 same 的另一種用法,專表示「我也是」的意思,當你的談話對手提出一個看法,或說明一件事之後,你可以很簡單地表示 Same here.「我跟你一樣」、「彼此、彼此」、「同病相憐」等意思。

### 句型 連結站

## Same for me.
給我相同的東西。

## Me too.
我也是;我也要。

## I agree.
我同意。

**A** Where are you going for spring break?

**B** I'm going to Hong Kong.

**A** Hey, **same** here.
When do you leave?

**B** As soon as my last class is over.

☑ spring break
春假

☑ break
[brek]
短假期

☑ as soon as
馬上

☑ over
['ovɚ]
結束

A 你春假要去什麼地方？

B 我要去香港。

A 嘿，我也是。
你什麼時候離開？

B 最後一節課一結束，我馬上就走。

203

# 097

# get together ~
聚在一起…

MP3-98

Let's **get together** for lunch.
讓我們聚在一起，吃個午餐吧。

---

### 句型解析站

　　朋友久沒見面，偶而相約見面，用 get together 聚在一起這個片語，要約朋友聚一聚，可以記 We need to get together. 或 Let's get together. 這兩個句型。

---

### 句型 連結站

We need to get together more often.
我們要更經常聚在一起才好。

Let's get together for a drink.
我們一起喝杯酒吧。

When are we going to get together and have some fun?
我們幾時可以聚一聚，好好的玩一玩呢？

**A** Let's **get together** for lunch next week.

**B** How about Tuesday at 11:30?

**A** Sounds good.
Is the cafeteria okay?

**B** Sure. I'll see you then.

☑ together
[tə'gɛðə]
一起

☑ drink
[drɪŋk]
飲料

☑ often
['ɔfən]
常常

☑ cafeteria
[kæfə'tɪrɪə]
自助餐廳

A 讓我們下星期聚在一起，吃午餐吧。

B 星期二的十一點半怎麼樣？

A 聽起來不錯。
吃自助餐可以嗎？

B 當然可以。我們到時候見。

205

MP3-99

# 098

# a piece of cake
易如反掌

It should be **a piece of cake** for you.
那對你來講，應該是易如反掌。

　　當我們要說某件事，或某個任務很簡單時，我們說那件事或那個任務是a piece of cake。「一塊蛋糕」在桌上，隨手拿來，好吃又容易下嚥的意思。

It won't be any trouble. It's a piece of cake.
那不會麻煩的。簡直是易如反掌。

This task should be a piece of cake for him.
這件工作對他來講，應該是易如反掌。

I don't see any problem with it. It should be just a piece of cake.
這件事我看不會有什麼問題。應該是易如反掌。

**A** I'm really worried about this test.

**B** Don't.
It should be **a piece of cake** for you.

**A** I know.
But the test weighs so much.

**B** Relax.
You know the material.

☑ cake
[kek]
蛋糕

☑ worried
['wɜɪd]
擔心的

☑ weigh
[we]
比重

☑ relax
[rɪ'læks]
放輕鬆點

☑ material
[mə'tɪrɪəl]
考試範圍

A 我對這次考試,非常擔心。

B 大可不必。
對你來講,應該是易如反掌。

A 我知道。
不過,這次考試的比重很重。

B 放輕鬆吧。
你對考試範圍都知道。
你一定可以考得很好的。

# 099

# How did you do on ~?

你…的表現如何？

MP3-100

句型 模擬站

## How did you do on your test?

你這一次考試考的如何？

### 句型解析站

問對方在某件事上表現得如何？因為那件事已經做了，所以問時要用過去式疑問句 How did you ~? 注意助動詞是did。

### 句型 連結站

How did you do on your contest?

你這一次比賽結果如何？

How did you do on your presentation?

你所做的簡報結果如何？

How did you do on your job?

你的工作表現如何？

**A** **How did you do on** your test?

**B** I got lucky on this one.
She didn't ask any questions over the material I didn't have a chance to go over.

**A** So you think you did well.

**B** I should have.

---

A 你這次考試的結果如何？

B 我這一次的運氣不錯。
她沒有問到我沒有準備的任何問題。

A 那麼你認為你考得很好囉。

B 我想是吧。

☑ test
[tɛst]
測驗

☑ contest
['kɑntɛst]
比賽

☑ presentation
[ˌprɛzn̩'teʃən]
簡報

☑ material
[mə'tɪrɪəl]
考試範圍

☑ go over
複習；溫習

# 100

## Is it okay to ~?
### 做…可以嗎？

MP3-101

## Is it okay to work together on it?
我們一起做這一件事好嗎？

這個句型裏的 it 是虛主詞，真正的主詞是後面的不定詞to work together on it. 所以，若問 Is it okay? 它可以嗎？要知道到底問那件事可以嗎？要去看後面的不定詞，真正是問to work together on it 可以嗎？

Is it okay to smoke in the office?
在辦公室裡抽煙可以嗎？

Is it okay to postpone it until tomorrow?
把它延期到明天，可以嗎？

Is it all right to stay up late?
晚上熬夜晚一點，可以嗎？

**A** Have you started your Accounting practice yet?

**B** No, have you?

**A** Not really.
I've looked at it
But I haven't gotten into it yet.

**B** It looks really difficult.
**Is it okay to** work together on it?

**A** I think so, but I'm not sure.

**B** Let's check with the professor.

**A** Sounds good.

A 會計學練習你開始做了嗎？

B 沒有，你呢？

A 不算真正開始。
我已經大約看了一下。
不過還沒有深入研究。

B 它看起來真的很困難。
我們一起來做可以嗎？

A 我想可以吧，不過我不是很確定。

B 那麼我們先問一下教授吧。

A 好吧。

☑ smoke
[smok]
抽煙

☑ postpone
[post'pon]
延期

☑ stay up
熬夜

☑ Accounting
[ə'kaʊntɪŋ]
會計學

☑ practice
['præktɪs]
練習

☑ difficult
['dɪfəˌkəlt]
困難的

☑ professor
[prə'fɛsɚ]
教授

MP3-102

# 101

# work
行得通

## Will that **work**?
那行得通嗎？

work 這個字在這裡的用法指「這樣做行得通」。若說「這樣做是行不通的」，可以說 That won't work. 或 I don't think that will work.。

That will work fine.
那一定行得通，沒問題。

That won't work.
那行不通的。

I don't think that will work.
我想那是行不通的。

**A** My car is in the shop.
Would you take me to pick it up?

☑ pick up
拿東西

**B** I can come over to your house at 5:30.
Will that **work**?

☑ shop
[ʃɑp]
店裏;修理廠

**A** That would be wonderful.
Thank you so much.

**B** No problem.
I'll see you then.

A 我的車子在修理廠裡。
你可以載我去把它拿回來嗎?

B 我五點半到你家來好了。
那樣子可以嗎?

A 那樣子太好了。
非常感謝你。

B 沒問題。
咱們到時見。

# *102*

## not ~ until ~
### 直到…才可以…

MP3-103

句型 模擬站

We **won't** know **until** it's announced.
直到宣佈以後，我們才會曉得。

句型解析站

　　說到 not ~ until ~這個用法，要注意中、英語法上的不同，中文的說法是「到什麼時候才會怎麼樣」，但英語卻用「We won't know（我們不會知道）until it's announced.（直到宣佈的時候。）」

句型 連結站

We can't get it done until tomorrow.
我們一直要到明天才做得完。

He won't be back until 3:00.
他要到3點才會回來。

They didn't leave until the rain stopped.
他們一直等到雨停了，才離開。

**A** It looks like Mary is going to get the promotion.

**B** Do you think so?
I thought Susan was going to.

**A** Really? I hadn't heard anything about her.

**B** Well, we **won't** know **until** it's announced.

☑ announce
　[ə'naʊns]
　宣佈

☑ promotion
　[prə'moʃən]
　升遷

☑ until
　[ən'tɪl]
　直到

A 看起來瑪麗會得到升遷。

B 你真的這樣認為嗎？
　我想蘇珊才會得到升遷。

A 真的嗎？我對於蘇珊，一點都沒聽說。

B 噢，我們要到宣佈以後才會知道吧。

# 103

## Be ~

務必…

### 句型 模擬站

**Be** back in thirty minutes.
務必在30分鐘之內回來。

#### 句型解析站

這個句型是命令句，主詞You省略掉， 詞必須用原形動詞Be。否定句用Don't be ~。

### 句型 連結站

Be good and have fun.
要乖，祝你玩得愉快。

Don't be a jerk.
不要那麼渾球好不好。

Be careful.
務必小心。

Be careful when you drive.
開車時請務必小心。

**A** May I go over to the playground?

**B** Have you finished your home-work and chores?

**A** I still have five math problems to do.
But I really need to take a break.

**B** All right.
But **be** back in thirty minutes.

☑ jerk
[dʒɝk]
混球

☑ go over to
去某個地方

☑ chore
[tʃor]
每日必做的雜務事

☑ take a break
休息一下

A 我可以到遊樂場玩嗎？

B 你的功課，和一些應該做的事都做完了嗎？

A 我還有五題數學題。
不過，我真的需要休息一下。

B 好吧。
務必要在三十分鐘內回來喲。

## 104 way too ~
### 簡直太…

MP3-105

**句型 模擬站**

There is **way too** much salt in this soup.

這個湯裡的鹽，簡直太多了。

**句型解析站**

way 這個字在口語中做副詞，用來強調後面的形容詞或副詞。常與 too 連用，強調 too，表示「簡直太……」。

**句型 連結站**

This is way too hard to do.
這個簡直是太難做了。

He is way behind in the race.
他在這場競賽之內，簡直落後太多了。

He's gone way too far.
他做的簡直太過份了。

**A** How is your meal?

----

**B** There is **way too** much salt in this soup.

----

**A** Really? Would you like something else instead?

----

**B** Yes, I think a salad would be good.

----

A 你點的菜如何？

B 這個湯裡的鹽，簡直太多了。

A 真的嗎？你要換點其他的嗎？

B 好吧，我想沙拉應該不錯。

☑ salt
　[sɔlt]
　鹽

☑ soup
　[sup]
　湯

☑ meal
　[mil]
　餐飲

☑ race
　[res]
　賽跑；競賽

☑ go too far
　太過份

☑ instead
　[ɪnˋstɛd]
　取代

MP3-106

# 105

## It involves a lot of ~

那要牽涉到很多…

**句型 模擬站**

## It involves a lot of statistics.

那需要很多的統計工作。

**句型解析站**

> 本句型在日常討論中，使用特別多，它用 involve 這個字，原意是「牽涉」，而真正含意是「需要」。所以講話中說 It involves...，就是需要後面那個點點所代表的事物。

**句型 連結站**

## It involves a lot of hard work.

那需要很多的辛勤工作。

## It involves a lot of money.

那需要很多錢。

## It involves a lot of labor.

那需要很多的工作。

**A** What are you doing your thesis on?

**B** I'm examining the relationship between interest rates and stock prices.

**A** Wow, that sounds rather complex.

**B** I guess.
**It involves a lot of** statistics.

**A** Well, you aced statistics so it should be a piece of cake for you.

**B** Fortunately we have a statistics software that will do all the calculations.
All I really have to do is develop the model.

---

A 你的論文主題是什麼？

B 我是探討利率與股票價格之間的關係。

A 哇，聽起來非常複雜。

B 我想是吧。
那要用到很多統計學。

A 是嗎，你的統計學太棒了，所以那對你來講，應該是易如反掌。

B 我們蠻幸運的有統計軟體可以做所有的計算。
我真正須要做的，是發展一套模式出來就行了。

☑ hard work
辛勤的工作

☑ labor
[ˈlebɚ]
勞力

☑ relationship
[rɪˈleʃənˌʃɪp]
關係

☑ complex
[kəmˈplɛks]
複雜的

☑ statistics
[stəˈtɪstɪks]
統計學

☑ model
[ˈmɑdl̩]
模式

☑ ace
[es]
精通

# 106

## in ~ favor
對…有利

MP3-107

**句型 模擬站**

That might be **in** your **favor**.
那可能對你有利。

---

**句型解析站**

favor 這個字是「有利、有益處」的意思。片語 in one's favor 就是「對某人有利」的意思，one's 可以用任何的所有格代替，例如，my（我的）、your（你的）、his（他的）、her（她的）、our（我們的）、your（你們的）、their（他們的）。

---

**句型 連結站**

The result might not be in my favor.
結果未必對我有利。

The weather is in our favor.
天氣對我們有利。

Be happy. The whole thing is in our favor.
高興一點吧。整個事情對我們很有利。

**A** Excuse me, Dr. Smith, I have a question about my exam grade.

**B** I would be happy to take a look at it. However, if I do, I re-grade the entire exam.

**A** What do you mean?

**B** If a student thinks the grader made an error, I will be happy to look at it.
However, I will look and see if other "errors" were made as well.
They include those that might be **in** your **favor**.

**A** Oh, that's fine.

---

A 對不起，史密斯博士，對於我的考試成績，我有問題。

B 我很樂意幫你看一下。
不過，如果我重看的話，我會整個試卷每一題都重看。

A 你是什麼意思？

B 如果有學生認為閱卷的人改錯了，我會很樂意再重看的。
不過，我也會重看是不是也犯了其他的「錯」。
包括那一些你原本錯的，我改成對的。

A 噢，那沒問題。

---

☑ favor
['fevɚ]
恩惠；益處

☑ result
[rɪ'zʌlt]
結果

☑ grade
[gred]
成績

☑ entire
[ɪn'taɪr]
全部的

☑ grader
['gredɚ]
閱卷的人

☑ error
['ɛrɚ]
錯誤

☑ include
[ɪn'klud]
包括

☑ as well
也；同時

國家圖書館出版品預行編目資料

流利英語必備句型 / 蘇盈盈 著. -- 新北市：哈福企業
有限公司, 2024.01
　　面；　　公分. -- (英語系列；86)
ISBN 978-626-98088-4-7 (平裝)
1.CST: 英語 2.CST: 句法
805.169　　　　　　　　　　　　112020077

**免費下載QR Code音檔**
行動學習，即刷即聽

# 流利英語必備句型
## （附QR碼線上音檔）

........................................................

作者／蘇盈盈
責任編輯／Charles Wang
封面設計／李秀英
內文排版／林樂娟
出版者／哈福企業有限公司
地址／新北市淡水區民族路 110 巷 38 弄 7 號
電話／(02) 2808-4587
傳真／(02) 2808-6545
郵政劃撥／31598840
戶名／哈福企業有限公司
出版日期／2024 年 1 月
台幣定價／379 元 ( 附線上 MP3)
港幣定價／126 元 ( 附線上 MP3)
封面內文圖／取材自 Shutterstock

........................................................

全球華文國際市場總代理／采舍國際有限公司
地址／新北市中和區中山路 2 段 366 巷 10 號 3 樓
電話／(02) 8245-8786 傳真／(02) 8245-8718
網址／ www.silkbook.com 新絲路華文網

........................................................

香港澳門總經銷／和平圖書有限公司
地址／香港柴灣嘉業街 12 號百樂門大廈 17 樓
電話／(852) 2804-6687
傳真／(852) 2804-6409

........................................................

email ／ welike8686@Gmail.com
facebook ／ Haa-net 哈福網路商城

電子書格式：PDF